"Everything's going to be okay, Waylon. Nothing has to change," Christina started.

The knot of nerves in his belly tightened. Now he was sure everything was about to flip on its head.

"My sister made a lot of mistakes. You know most of them. Heck, you were the victim of most of her poor decisions," Christina continued, as she ran her fingers over the back of his hand. "But, there was one mistake... Well, not mistake, but rather an *error in judgment* that...well... We all... We..."

"We are just as much at fault as Alli," his mother said, her voice high with nerves. "We should have told you sooner. Years ago, but—"

"Wait," he said, with a raise of the hand. "*What* exactly should you have told me years ago?"

"It's about Winnie..." Christina began.

His heart stopped at the sound of the little girl's name.

Christina looked up at him and her eyes were filled with a look of apologetic fear. "Winnie is yours, Waylon. She's your daughter."

Mr Serious

DANICA WINTERS

First Published in Great Britain 2017
By Mills & Boon, an imprint of HarperCollins*Publishers*
1 London Bridge Street, London, SE1 9GF

Large Print edition 2017

ISBN: 978-0-263-07243-3

MIX
Paper from
responsible sources
FSC
www.fsc.org   FSC™ C007454

This book is produced from independently certified FSC paper to ensure responsible forest management. For more information visit www.harpercollins.co.uk/green.

Printed and bound in Great Britain
by CPI Group (UK) Ltd, Croydon, CR0 4YY

Danica Winters is a multiple award-winning, bestselling author who writes books that grip readers with their ability to drive emotion through suspense and occasionally a touch of magic. When she's not working, she can be found in the wilds of Montana, testing her patience while she tries to hone her skills at various crafts—quilting, pottery and painting are not her areas of expertise. She believes the cup is neither half-full nor half-empty, but it better be filled with wine. Visit her website at danicawinters.net.

To Mac.

You're the mac to my cheese
and the butter to my bread.

Thanks for making life
such an amazing adventure.

Acknowledgements

This series wouldn't have been possible without a great team of people, including my editors at Mills & Boon – thank you for all your hard work.

Also, thank you to Suzanne Miller and the crew at Dunrovin Ranch in Lolo, Montana. Suzanne is the inspiration behind one of my favourite characters in this series, the fantastic Eloise Fitzgerald. Just like Eloise, she always greets you with a warm smile and an open heart.

Chapter One

It was Waylon Fitzgerald's firm belief that most people were the same when it came to their wants. People were driven to desire four major things: good-enough sex, at least a comfortable amount of money, to be happy most of the time and to find someone to love them. Lucky for him, he'd never been like most people. His dreams were so much bigger—he wanted it all, and more. He wanted to travel the world, to help those in need, to live the dream and have a life driven by passion—not by *good enough*.

The helicopter's headset crackled to life.

"Where do you want me to put her down?" The pilot motioned out the window of the Black Hawk as they passed over the stock pond in the pasture where his mother normally put the horses out this time of year.

His family wasn't going to like that he was bringing the helicopter to the ranch, but thanks to the disappearance of his ex-wife, Waylon had had to catch the next available flight. As luck would have it, his friend was relocating bases from Fort Bragg to Fort Lewis and he got to come along for the ride.

He'd always loved the feel of the chopper, its blades cutting through the air and the thump they made, just like the thump of a heart. Maybe that was what the chopper and the army were— his heart. He glanced down at Dunrovin Ranch and the guesthouses speckled throughout its expanse.

As much as he had loved the place where

he spent most of his childhood, the lifestyle it symbolized was exactly what he feared the most—boredom. A life spent in habitual motion. Feed the horses, take care of the guests, take care of the ranch's maintenance, take care of the animals and go to bed, ready to repeat it every day until one morning he just didn't wake up. It wasn't that he judged his adoptive mother and father, Eloise and Merle Fitzgerald, for their need for complete stability. It was because of their stability and values he had even made it out of childhood alive. He owed them everything.

"Waylon?" the pilot asked again. "You got a place?"

"Put her down just there." He motioned toward the gravel parking lot that stood empty in the midmorning sun.

That was strange. This time of year, Dunrovin was normally hopping with life—winter-themed weddings, riding classes and parties to celebrate the coming of Christmas.

As the pilot lowered the bird toward the ground, people started spilling out of the main house. His adoptive mother waved at the helicopter, and even from a distance, he could see the smile on her face. In just the few years since he'd left the ranch, she'd grown gray and her back had started to take on the slight curve that came with age and osteoporosis. His father, the quiet and stoic man who was always working, stood beside her, holding her hand.

Next to them was a blonde. She was tall and lean, the body of a rider, but he didn't recognize her. She turned slightly, and he could make out the perfect round curve of her ass in her tight blue jeans. Perhaps she was one of their trainers. Either way, he'd have to watch out for her. She looked like the kind of woman who would end up in one of two positions with him—

either toe to toe in a shouting match, or between the sheets. As it was, he just needed to get in and out of the ranch and back to work. The last thing he needed was any more drama than necessary.

The blonde shaded her eyes as she frowned up at him, but after a moment her gaze moved to the apple tree in the corner of the lot. Standing high in its branches was a little girl who looked to be about three years old. Her brunette curls blowing in the rotor wash as she gawked at him.

What in the hell was a girl that little doing standing in a tree?

The blonde jogged toward her as if she'd had the same thought.

"Be careful," Waylon said to the pilot, pointing to the toddler.

The pilot pulled back on the stick, and the

powerful draft at such a low altitude kicked up a thick cloud of dust.

The little girl in the tree started to sway, and Waylon called out a warning into the deafening roar of the chopper's wash.

The girl trembled as she struggled to keep hold of the bark. She looked up at him as a gust of wind set her off balance, and her left shoe slid from the branch. The girl's blue dress moved against her like an unwieldy sail and propelled her out of the tree. She careened toward the ground.

From where he sat, it looked as though she landed face-first at the bottom of the tree.

"Bring this bird down, dammit!" he shouted.

Hopefully the little girl was still alive.

Chapter Two

What kind of man thought it was okay to fly into a quiet ranch like he was some kind of freaking hero? Who did Waylon Fitzgerald think he was? All that man ever did was leave destruction in his wake, and as far as Christina Bell was concerned, this was just another example of how little he cared when it came to how his actions affected others.

She rushed to her niece as the girl tumbled out of the apple tree and landed on the ground. The girl let out a shrill cry, but it was nearly drowned out by the chopping of the blades of the bull-in-a-china-shop helicopter.

"Winnie, are you okay?" Christina called above the sound.

Tears streamed down Winnie's dusty face, cutting through the dirt and exposing her unmarred skin below. "It hurts."

"It's okay, Win. You'll be okay." Christina ran her hand over the girl's head, smoothing her curls and trying to comfort her. "Where does it hurt, sweetie?"

Winnie cried, and her sobs stole her voice, but she motioned to her right arm and wrist. Of course it would be the girl's arm. She'd probably put her hand down during her fall in an attempt to catch herself.

As soon as the helicopter touched down, Waylon ran over, dropping his bag on the ground at Winnie's feet. "Are you okay, kid?"

Christina turned toward him, and she could feel a snarl take over her face. "You leave her alone."

He took two steps back, like he was afraid a bite would follow the growl. It might have been the smartest thing he'd done so far. All she wanted to do was come at him. He was the reason Winnie was hurt—in many ways, he was responsible for the bad things in her life.

She stared at him as the helicopter lifted off the ground and set to the sky. Alli had told her that he was a military police officer for the army, and she had seen pictures of him in the main house, but none of that did him justice. The man, all two hundred-ish pounds of him, was lean, and from what she could see, his chest was just as muscular as his legs. Even his forearms were thick, so much so that the muscles stressed the cloth of his rolled-up plaid sleeves.

He gave her a small smile, like he hoped that it would be his get-out-of-jail-free card, and she forced herself to look away from his almond-shaped eyes, buzzed black hair and copper-toned skin. He was a far cry from the scraggly teenager whose pictures adorned Eloise Fitzgerald's walls. Christina didn't like him, but she couldn't deny he might have been one of the sexiest men she'd ever seen in real life. She could certainly understand how her sister had fallen for the man. And regardless of Alli's latest drama, she had been right in divorcing the man if his entrance was any indication of his character.

Just because a man was ridiculously handsome and knew how to make an entrance, it didn't make him a man worth calling a husband—or a father.

Yep, she definitely hated him. Maybe it was just her hatred of every man who'd left his wife in the lurch, or it could have been all the things Alli had told her about the guy, but there was nothing redeemable about him. Not even that stupid grin he tried to ply her with.

"Is the kid okay?" he asked, his rough voice suddenly taking on a silky edge.

It wouldn't work with her. No way. No how. Especially when he referred to his daughter as "the kid," but then again, he didn't know who she was to him.

Winnie looked up at the man and wiped the tears from her cheeks with her good hand. "My arm," she said, lifting her limp right arm for him to see. "It hurts."

He squatted down next to Christina, far too close. He smelled like motor oil and spicy men's cologne—if she had to explain it, she would have said it was the scent of a real man. On the other hand, it was the scent of Waylon Fitzgerald—notorious father at large.

He didn't reach for the girl; instead, he leaned

back on his heels as though being that close to a hurt child made him deeply uncomfortable.

"Does your back hurt, sweetie?" Christina asked.

Winnie shook her head and stood up, being careful not to put any weight on her arm. The area around her wrist was red and had already started to take on a faint bruise. It had to be broken, yet amazingly the little girl had stopped crying.

"What's your name, kid?" Waylon asked.

"Winnie. I gonna be three."

"You're such a big girl." He looked over at Christina. "Is she yours?"

She snorted at how ridiculous his question was. "I'm her guardian."

Waylon frowned as though he was trying to connect the dots. "So you are…"

She ignored his question. As far as she was concerned, he didn't need to know her. He'd missed his chance to know her and her family when he'd chosen to elope with Alli. He'd never cared before—and he didn't need to start now.

Eloise and Merle Fitzgerald made their way over to them as the helicopter disappeared into the distance. Eloise looked torn between worry and excitement. "Waylon!" she called, waving. "Hey, kiddo!"

Christina stood and wrapped Winnie in her arms, holding her against her legs as she chuckled at Eloise's welcome—calling Waylon a kiddo was about as fitting as calling a wolf a Chihuahua.

Waylon didn't look back at them as he made his way over to his mother and gave her a solid hug and a quick peck to the cheek. He turned to his father and shook the man's hand. Apparently, Waylon was the serious kind, a guy who was all business. His father deserved a hug—

even if Waylon thought he was too much of a man for that kind of thing.

She sighed as she thought of all the reasons she had to keep the secret about Winnie from him. He definitely wouldn't be as good a parent as she was—and Winnie deserved the best care she could get.

Eloise glanced over at her and, almost as though she could read Christina's mind, gave her a slight raise of the brow before she knelt down to talk to Winnie. "You gonna be okay, pumpkin? That was a pretty big fall, but you were so brave."

"Nana, I tough." Winnie smiled, the action tight from pain, but thankfully Eloise's compliments were taking her mind off her arm.

"Nana?" Waylon interrupted.

"Oh, yeah." Eloise waved him off, but from the way she didn't answer her son's question, Christina could tell that she was also questioning exactly if, how and when they should give him the news. Eloise turned back to Winnie. "Let's go see Dr. Richards. I bet he would like to hear about how brave you were. Okay, pumpkin?"

"I want Wy-ant." Winnie said, giving Eloise her special brand of puppy-dog eyes—the ones that worked on everyone who lived at the ranch and especially Christina.

For a brief second, Christina felt guilty for not telling Waylon then and there about Winnie being his. It wasn't really her secret to tell, and even if it were, the revelation would change everything—he would likely want to step into his role as a father and take Winnie away from Dunrovin. Even the thought of more change broke her heart.

She glanced over at him, hoping he would crack a smile—anything that would make him seem like a man who deserved to be Winnie's guardian. He just looked back at her, a solemn look on his face. So much for that.

Perhaps all she could hope for was that he wouldn't want to take the girl away. Maybe he would want his daughter to stay at the ranch while he continued to roam the world, but it wasn't a risk she was willing to take. She loved the girl entirely too much to risk her future on Mr. Serious and a life that he most likely didn't want.

"I'll call Wyatt," Christina offered, but in truth it was just an excuse to get away from the infuriatingly handsome army man.

Sometimes, when things were this confusing, the only thing to do was run.

ALL WAYLON WANTED to do was get out of this place. He hated hospitals. Thanks to his time in Iraq, there was no place he dreaded more.

If a guy was in the hospital there, bad things had gone down.

Truth be told, in Iraq, the name of the game was bad things.

Every second there was another enemy, another battle to fight, another person to protect. And here, back in the civilian world, no one seemed to understand how ugly the real world was. Waylon's brother Wyatt tapped his foot as he sat next to him in the waiting room, agitated that they hadn't been invited to the examination room with Winnie, where they were going over the results of the X-rays.

"She'll be okay, man," Waylon said. "Kids are resilient. And, honestly, except for the bruise, she seemed fine. Who knows, maybe her wrist ain't broken."

Wyatt nodded. "That kid's tougher than you think. If she cried, there had to be something majorly wrong. I've seen her get stepped on by a horse and barely bat an eyelash."

He'd nearly forgotten how tough even the youngest members of the family were expected to be. There was no time for weakness when they were out checking on cattle during calving season or when they were breaking a new horse. If there was weakness, animals would sense it, and undoubtedly use it to their advantage. The ability to disguise pain was a vital part of existence out here in the wilds of Montana, where it often came down to survival of the fittest. Since he'd left three years ago after his divorce, he'd barely thought about the ranch—and he had completely forgotten how much Mystery, Montana, felt like a throwback to a bygone era. It really was a different culture, a tiny microcosm of society where the values revolved around family and community.

It was a different world than the one he'd been in overseas.

It surprised him, but for a moment, a feeling of sadness and nostalgia overtook him. He hadn't realized how much he'd missed home. Well, he'd missed *some* things about home. He glanced over toward the door that led to the examination rooms, where the blonde and his mother were with Winnie. The blonde seemed to hate his guts. When he took off again, he'd miss a lot of things, but her hate wasn't one of them.

Hopefully he had time to make her change her mind about him—he'd overcome worse odds with women before. Heck, Alli had really hated him when they'd first met. She had been waiting tables at the little diner in Mystery, the Combine, making money before moving along to the next town. The first time she'd seen him, he could have cut glass with her sharp glare.

He'd loved that about Alli, the way she was so strong and always ready to stand up for herself. So many women just let men walk all over them, but not Alli. Then again, it was that same strength that had pushed him away and led her into the arms of another man, and then another, and another.

"Have you heard anything new about Alli?" Waylon asked, trying not to notice the way his gut clenched when he thought about all the hard times he'd gone through with the woman.

Wyatt shifted in his standard-issue plastic hospital chair. "They have her car at the impound lot. We're holding it until we get the full forensics report. But thanks to Lyle, it may take a while."

"Lyle is still working for you guys? Can't you find anyone better?" he teased his brother, but he knew exactly how it worked with small-town politics—where the good ole boy system was still alive and well.

"Lyle isn't all bad," Wyatt said with a laugh. "Though he probably could use a refresher course or two. He did find the photos that pointed us toward Alli in the case of Bianca's murder."

"Even a blind squirrel finds a nut once in a while."

"You got that right." Wyatt's laughter echoed through the nearly empty waiting room. "If you want, when we're done here, we can run up to her car. Maybe you can spot something we've missed. Though, I gotta say, there ain't a whole lot there."

"Maybe you just needed your little brother to come home and show you how to do *real* investigative work. Like we do in the military," Waylon said with a booming laugh.

"Is that what they're calling the Girl Scouts these days?" Wyatt smirked.

It was moments like these, when his belly hurt from laughter, that made him realize being home wasn't just about a change of location. It was more about family—and family was something he could never replace.

Chapter Three

Waylon was certain he shouldn't feel guilty for the state of Winnie, yet he couldn't help the tug at his heart each time he looked at her clunky, Ace bandage–wrapped arm as they all made their way into the main house. Dr. Richards had said it was only a sprain, but just to be sure he hadn't missed a microscopic crack, Eloise and the girl's guardian had gone along with his plan to keep it wrapped for at least the next week.

Waylon followed the blonde woman toward the kitchen as Winnie pushed past. The woman had barely spoken to him since they had left the hospital. *Pissed* didn't even seem like a strong enough word to express the vibe she was sending his way. It was going to be a long week at the ranch. He'd thought war zones were bad, but at least there he wasn't the sole focus of a woman's wrath.

His mother stepped up beside him, and as she noticed him watching the woman, she chuckled. "Don't worry about Christina—she'll come around. She's just a bit protective of Winnie, that's all."

"Christina?" He let out a long breath. "As in Alli's sister, Christina?"

"The one and only. She's been a real asset to the ranch. Didn't you recognize her?"

He'd only ever seen pictures of Alli's sister. Alli had made sure to keep him at arm's length from her family—when he had suggested having them at their wedding, it was in that moment Alli unilaterally decided they should elope. He should have seen it as a warning that she had some issues, but no, love had made him blind. So blind he hadn't noticed when she had started to keep him isolated; after a couple of years he never saw his friends or even his brothers.

If he'd been smarter, he would have seen what she was really doing—using him to take care of her while she pursued another man. As much as he had the right to, he didn't hate her. Emotions were crazy, and love was even more illogical. Not that he still loved her. No. That feeling had died the moment he'd left the ranch and run away to the military. The day he signed his papers was the day he had let his past go—that was, until now.

Christina turned around, standing in the doorway of the kitchen, and glared at him. "For some reason, Winnie is asking about you. You may want to go see her."

He could almost hear the hiss in her words. Yep, she hated him. *Sweet.*

He sighed, and his mother gave his arm a little squeeze. "Don't worry, kiddo. I'm telling you, her bark's worse than her bite."

He had a feeling he would get the chance to see if his mother was right, but if Christina's attitude toward him was any indication of her bite, he was sure he'd come away with at least a mark or two.

Winnie sat at the table while Wyatt set about grabbing supplies for a peanut butter and jelly sandwich. As he walked to the table, Wyatt turned to Waylon. "Want one?" He lifted the jelly. "This is what you eat for lunch in the Girl Scouts, right?" His brother laughed.

Stepping behind Winnie so she couldn't see, he flipped his brother the bird. "It's still better than a solid diet of doughnuts, Deputy." He rubbed his stomach. "In fact, I think you're growing a bit around the middle."

Wyatt laughed. "You need to move back to the ranch."

"You looking for someone to help you with your *Dumb and Dumber* act?" Waylon teased.

The girl wiggled in her chair. "Yeah, Way-lawn." She said his name like she had to think about each syllable on its own, and it made it sound like a children's rhyme. "You come back. And you know what? We have party."

Waylon chuckled. "Is that right?"

"Uh-huh," she said with an overly exaggerated nod. "Way-lawn, you and me, we dress up. You help me?"

He'd had bullets whiz by his head in active combat zones, and he'd stepped in front of high-value dignitaries, ready to give his life for the greater good, yet, as Winnie looked up at him, he couldn't help the fear that rose within him.

He had no idea what to do with a kid—especially a kid who wanted to do a craft project. Maybe he'd have more of a clue if she wanted to strip down an assault rifle, but costumes— he was totally out of his league.

Christina gave a wry laugh from behind him. "Waylon doesn't do that kind of thing, sweetheart. If you want, though, I can help you later."

He noted the jab she was taking at him, and he couldn't help rising to the fight. "Nah, Ms. Winnie. Don't you worry, I got you. You want a costume? I'm your man." His stomach clenched as he thought about how ill equipped he was for the promise he'd just made.

"Don't you have a *job* to do? You know, trying to find my missing, fugitive sister? Or are you going to just let her get away with murdering the vet and William Poe's wife?" Christina rebuked.

She stared at him, and some of the anger that

had filled her features seemed to melt away, re-placed by shame. "Look, I'm sorry," she said, not waiting for him to talk. "I didn't mean it like that. I'm just…just…"

"Hurting," he said, finishing her thought.

She sighed, not admitting he was right, but he could see from the way her posture softened that he'd hit the truth. Of course she would be hurting and scared, and probably overwhelmed. Her sister was her only family, since their mother had passed away a few years back.

"I want to find her. Alli needs to come home," she said, her gaze moving to Winnie and the bandage on her arm.

What was he missing? There was something happening that they weren't telling him—he could feel it in the air.

"What's going on?" he asked, tired of skirting the issue.

"Huh?" Christina looked up at him, a look

of shock flashing over her features. "What do you mean?"

"You guys are hiding something." He turned to Wyatt, who all of a sudden seemed wholly consumed by the process of making another sandwich. "What is it that you don't want me to know?"

His mother walked into the kitchen, almost as if the question had beckoned her to the room. She glanced around at Christina and Wyatt, as if giving them some signal. "Everything's fine, kiddo. We're all just worried about Alli."

"Did she do something you aren't telling me? I mean, besides murdering Bianca and that other woman and then going on the run?"

His mother smiled. "It's not what she did but what she didn't do that is the problem."

"What's that supposed to mean?"

His mother touched his shoulder. "Just work

on finding Alli. Then we can deal with everything else."

Some of the fondness he was feeling toward being home drifted away. He'd forgotten how the family always turned inward first—and because of his time away, he now stood outside the circle.

"Look, why don't we run over to the impound lot?" Wyatt said, waving the peanut butter–laden knife around in the air.

"You're not leaving me here alone to wonder what's going on," Christina pressed, but she glanced over at his mother with a question in her eyes.

"Don't worry, I'll watch Winnie," Eloise offered.

Whatever was going on revolved around that little girl. Waylon glanced at Winnie. How was she involved with all of this? Was it possible she was Alli's daughter? Was that why there was such a rush to find the woman—and why they had been adamant that he come home to help them in the search? He pushed the thoughts from his mind. Alli had always told him she was unable to get pregnant. The child couldn't be hers.

THE IMPOUND LOT was attached to the prerelease center on the outskirts of town. It wasn't much of a place. Wyatt punched in his key code, and the gate of the chain link–enclosed lot opened with a grinding sound. There was a collection of beat-up old cars and one late-model Mustang. Most of the jalopies had flat tires or shattered windshields, and more than a few had both. The lot even had a few campers that looked like they'd escaped the show *Breaking Bad*, complete with what Waylon was sure were meth labs inside.

He chuckled, but his humor was short-lived

as they drove around the corner and came into view of the convicts' exercise yard. One of the prisoners looked over, and as he caught sight of Wyatt's patrol unit, he spat on the ground and flipped them the bird. As the other prisoners noticed, the middle finger came in almost a concert-style wave, rippling through the yard.

"Nothing quite like the royal welcome, right?" Wyatt said, ignoring his fan club.

"I'm acquainted with the lifestyle," Waylon said with a cynical laugh.

Christina tapped her fingers on the car door. "That's what you guys get all the time? No wonder you both have chips on your shoulders."

He and his brother looked at each other and shared a smug grin. A few middle fingers were nothing compared to facing down a drunk man with a gun who wanted to kill him for some past injustice he felt he had suffered at the hands of the police. It was a strange feeling to know that most of the time, wherever he went, people despised him.

Sure, it was true most of the population weren't criminals, but the people they worked with every day weren't the general public—in his case, the criminals he worked with were even worse than Wyatt's. For Waylon, when he was working on a base between deployments to war zones, the people he arrested were well trained in weapons and self-defense—his job was to handle trained killers. Wyatt just had to handle drunken idiots.

Wyatt parked his car next to a black Hyundai Genesis. "It was pretty beat-up by the time we got the report that it had been abandoned. You know how that goes," his brother said, motioning toward the wreckage.

The car had a flat tire on the passenger's side, and its windshield was shattered. For a moment, Waylon imagined Alli's car on the side of the road, people smashing it just because they could. People had a strange, innate need to destroy things that stood alone or abandoned. It was almost as though anonymity was enough justification for them to give license to their destructive nature.

"I went over this car with Lyle, top to bottom," Wyatt said, getting out and walking toward Alli's car.

"What all did you find?"

Wyatt shrugged. "We ran fingerprints, but nothing came of them. And all we found inside was the normal crap—wadded straw wrappers and a few fries under the seats."

"But nothing that you think would help us figure out where she could have gone?" Christina asked.

Wyatt looked over at her. "You and I both know she's in Canada somewhere. She's probably watching a hockey game, drinking Molson and laughing at how stupid she thinks we are."

"She's not like that. She knows you aren't stupid. She just got herself into a bad spot, and it escalated. I don't condone what she did, but there has to be more to it than we know. She had her problems, but I never thought she was capable of…you know," Christina said. She looked down at the ground with what Waylon assumed was shame.

He wanted to tell her he was just as confused and upset a woman he had once loved had made such a stupid series of decisions, but there was no making any of what Alli did better. There was only bringing her back so she could pay for her crimes—and so he could ask her all the questions he was dying to ask. He just couldn't understand how she had fallen into such a pit of self-destruction. Sure, she had never been exactly healthy, but he'd never thought she was capable of taking a life.

Then again, if he'd learned anything on the battlefield and as an MP, it was that all people were capable of pulling a trigger if the conditions were right.

"I'm sure when we find her we can get to the bottom of this," Waylon said in his best attempt to make Christina feel better. From the tired look on her face, he had failed.

"So," Wyatt said, opening the car's door, "we did find a receipt on the floor on the passenger's side. We tracked it down—it was to a gas station just outside Mystery. Alli filled up with gas, but beyond that there wasn't anything usable."

Waylon stepped beside his brother and leaned over the passenger's seat. The car was filled with the dirty, stale scent of the long neglected. He pulled the odor deep into his lungs. Over the years he had been around more than his fair share of abandoned vehicles that had been left behind by people on the run. The one scent the car didn't carry was the putrid odor of death. Its absence was really the only thing they had going for them—at least, for now.

He opened up the glove box. It was empty.

"We took all her documents out. They are in evidence, but there really wasn't anything unusual, just her insurance card and registration."

He closed it. "Huh." He stared at the headliner for a second.

Almost as if it were a sign, a wayward fly crawled out from behind the black felt. He reached up and ran his fingers along the edge of the liner. It gaped where the bug had exited. His fingers brushed against something rough—paper.

He pulled the paper out and held it in his hands as he stared at the thing in disbelief.

"You went through the whole car, huh?" He lifted the paper high for his brother to see.

"What's that?" Wyatt asked, his mouth open slightly with shock. "I swear, we went over this thing from top to bottom."

It was total dumb luck Waylon had found the paper. It was almost like the proverbial needle in the haystack, but he wouldn't admit that to his big brother. "Hold up your hand," Waylon said with a mischievous grin.

Wyatt frowned, but he played along, lifting his hand and extending his fingers.

"Oh, yep," Waylon said. "It's those stubby fingers that are the problem. You just couldn't reach it."

Wyatt balled his fingers into a tight fist, but he laughed. "Real funny, jackass. You just got lucky and you know it. In fact, it probably got loosened up when they towed the car."

"Wait," Christina said, "if you guys are done

picking at each other, what is on it? Is it from Alli?"

Waylon opened the folded page. Inside was a note in Alli's jagged, hurried scrawl. All it said was "I'm sorry. But, William, I don't understand. Why?"

It was almost as if while she had been writing the note, she had been interrupted and she had stuffed it half written in the headliner. What in the hell was it supposed to mean? And why would she leave such an obscure note behind? Had she meant for them to find it, or was it meant for someone else?

He thought he didn't hate Alli, but in this moment, the feeling threatened to overwhelm him.

Christina glanced over her shoulder and he could hear her breath catch.

"That doesn't make any sense," Christina said, mimicking his thoughts. "What did she mean by 'I don't understand'? She's the one who started all of this mess. She set the rules to this game."

He handed the note over to Wyatt. His brother shook his head and slipped it into his pocket. "I'll get this into evidence, but I have a feeling it's going to be just about as helpful as the straw wrappers. Do you remember William Poe?"

Waylon had met the county tax appraiser a time or two in passing, but aside from Poe's relationship with Alli and a brief mention of him in the newspapers thanks to the murder of his wife, Monica, Waylon didn't know much about the man.

Waylon shook his head.

"Poe is like a greased pig," Wyatt said. "Just when I think I can pin him down for something, he slips out of my grasp. I thought for sure he was involved with Bianca's and Monica's murders, but the guy always has an alibi. Always."

"And from what I hear, it usually involves politics or a woman's thighs," Christina added.

Wyatt laughed. "And sometimes a combination of the two."

"Did you check his alibi?" Waylon asked.

Wyatt looked at him with a raise of the brow. "Really? Dude, I'm not completely incompetent at my job."

He instantly regretted asking his brother such a stupid question. Of course Wyatt knew what he was doing—Waylon hadn't meant to step on his toes, but he was just so used to working alone, or rather, being in command, that coming here and being second in line in the investigation was out of his comfort zone.

"Boys, boys, you are both good at your jobs. Wyatt, I don't think that's what your brother meant," Christina said, trying to smooth the ground between them. "Right, Waylon?" She put her hand on his shoulder and gave it a light squeeze.

"Of course. Sorry, man."

Waylon stood up, and Christina's fingers slipped from him. He looked back at her, and he couldn't help but notice the way the midday sun made her normally icy blue eyes sparkle with warmth.

He forced himself to look away and walked toward the back of the car, stopping by the rear tire on the passenger's side. As he looked down, something odd caught his eye. "Wyatt," he said, squatting down and pressing his finger against a deformation in the rim's surface, "look at this."

Wyatt came over. "It's just a rock chip." But he knelt down beside him.

"No." Waylon pressed. "Look closer. That, Wyatt…is a bullet hole."

Chapter Four

Wyatt dropped them off at the ranch so Christina could get her truck and they could set to work. She sent a quick glance over at Waylon. His copper-toned skin glistened in the midday sun, and she couldn't help the little wiggle of attraction that rose up from her core.

Seeing him in his element, working over the car and finding what the rest had missed, had made some of the anger she had been carrying for the man fall to the wayside. He was good at his job, and he looked even better doing it.

This would have been so much easier if she

could just stay firmly planted in her dislike. It made it easier to compartmentalize and keep him as an enemy. Yet every time he joked around, she was tempted to think of him almost as a friend.

He turned to her as Wyatt drove off. "You sure you don't mind driving me around? I could just borrow one of the ranch's trucks. You don't have to keep me company."

She appreciated the out, but her whole body pushed her to stay with him. "I'm doing this for Alli. I can't stop looking just because you're here."

"Have you been looking for her nonstop since she went missing last week?" he asked. A frown crossed over his face, like he was surprised she had not given up.

"Of course. She's my sister. I don't have to agree with what she does, or the choices she makes, but I love her and I want to make sure that she's safe."

"If she called or you found her, do you think you'd be able to turn her in to the authorities— or Wyatt?"

She chewed on her lip. She'd already thought about that question, but she had pushed it to the back of her mind. "I need to know she's safe first, then I'll make that choice."

"Does that mean you would let her stay on the run?"

Alli deserved to pay for her crimes. She had murdered, but Christina had to think about Winnie, too. The girl was already bearing the weight of her mother's choices. If Alli went to prison, Winnie would have to visit that terrible place, but if Alli stayed on the run, things could be kept from Winnie until she was old enough to understand a bit better.

"Like I said, I'll make that choice when I'm faced with it," she said. "All I want now is to know that she's alive and well."

Waylon glanced down at his hands. "You know what? I get it," he said, looking at his tanned and calloused fingers. "Your sister has a good heart. I don't know why she acted like she did, but that doesn't mean I don't care about her and what happens to her. I want her to be safe—just like you do."

The way he spoke about Alli was endearing and completely unexpected. Alli had never spoken of him with anything close to the same warmth. In fact, if Christina had to guess, regardless of what Alli had told her, it was not a breakup he had instigated. If anything, it seemed like he might still have had feelings for her sister when they had split and maybe even now.

Which made the feelings Christina was starting to have for him all that much more wrong. How could she possibly be attracted to her sister's ex-husband? There was something so day-time gossip show about the whole thing.

She chuckled at the thought.

"What's so funny?" Waylon asked.

"I wasn't laughing at you," she said, trying to backpedal from her bad timing. "It's just that…" She couldn't tell him she was laughing about the way she was starting to feel about him.

"What?" he asked, spurring her on.

"It's just that I think we're one step away from being asked to be on the *Maury* show." She covered her mouth as she laughed and, as she did, the look of pain on Waylon's face disappeared and he smiled. It was filled with a jovial warmth, and there was even a look of something else in his eyes…something that resembled attraction.

Nope. She had to have it all wrong. There was no way he could be attracted to her.

"I…er…" she said. There was a faint warmth in her cheeks, and she tried to keep it in check. She walked toward her truck with him at her side. "I don't mean your family. Your mom and dad are great. It's just with the murders and everything…you know."

He motioned that it was okay for her to stop her rambling. "It's okay. I get it. And though my parents' lives are in order, you and I both know the same can't be said for the rest of us. That's without even mentioning this thing with Alli." He paused. "I can't even begin to imagine what she told you about me over the years." He glanced over at her, as if trying to gauge her reaction.

She bit the inside of her cheek. Alli had made a personal habit of ripping her ex-husband to shreds. Alli hadn't done it in front of Winnie as she had wanted to keep Winnie's father's identity a secret from her, but that didn't change the fact that over the years, some of the things she had told Christina had begun to wear her down and made her dislike him on principle.

"Yeah, I thought so," he said, as though he could read her mind. "Listen, Alli and I had a *tough* relationship." He said the word like it tasted of spoiled shellfish. "We never should have gotten married. I just thought that what we had was what love was supposed to be. I supported her—emotionally, mentally, even physically sometimes. It only made sense that we took the leap and made things official. But as soon as we got married, it was like a switch flipped. She went from bad to worse."

Christina should have been offended that he was saying her sister was bad, but she really didn't have a platform to argue anything different. Alli made poor choices on a regular basis.

"I thought I could handle her mood swings, but in the end—when she started sleeping with other men—I just couldn't have her in my life anymore. We weren't good together. We never were. It was just time that I left. She's the reason I went back to active duty. And you know what? I'm glad that I left. It was far better than letting your sister rip my soul apart."

His candor came as a surprise, so much so that Christina didn't quite know how to react. She should have stood up for her sister, yet at the same time, she could feel for Waylon. Her sister had a way of tearing down the people she loved. It was just a part of her personality, as if by pushing away the people she loved the most, she could protect herself from being vulnerable or at the mercy of others' feelings. It was almost as though she wanted to hurt them before they had the chance to hurt her.

It undoubtedly came from their childhood. Their parents had been emotional train wrecks—a world of constant cheating and berating. It was the reason Christina had sworn off men for the last few years. She had come too close to following in her parents' footsteps. Not loving was just so much easier than living a life like that of her childhood.

"Alli had her fair share of problems, and maybe a few extra, too," she said, giving him a knowing smile.

"I have mine, too," he said, making the desire she was feeling for him even more intense.

Waylon wasn't a perfect man, but Alli had been wrong when she'd told her that he didn't have a heart. Even now, when he had the chance to make Alli the fall guy, he took his lumps.

She threw him her truck keys. "Remember how to get around?"

His face pinched. "This old town ain't that big. I think I can remember where the Poe place is." He got into the driver's seat and revved the old truck to life.

Christina laughed as she slid onto the truck's bench seat—far too close to the man who was starting to make her heart do strange things. "You got that right." Sometimes, just like this truck, the town was entirely too small for comfort.

"Why did you come here?" he asked as he steered the truck onto the road. "I mean, no offense or anything, but there's so many amazing places in the world—places where anything you want is at your fingertips. Why would you, a woman in her late-twenties who could have anything—and anyone she wanted—come to a place like this and stay?"

Did he really think she could have anyone she wanted? She almost laughed at the thought.

The only men who had ever seemed to be attracted to her were emotional nitwits. They were just too much like her father—wanting her when it was convenient for them, and then forgetting about her when it wasn't.

She refused to chase another man. She wasn't the kind of woman who pursued men and made things fit when they truly didn't. She wanted the elusive unicorn—the kind of guy who actually made the effort, the kind who wanted her for her and not what she had between her legs, and the kind who fit into her life naturally instead of feeling like a fish out of water.

She glanced over at Waylon as he drove. He would fit right in. It was his family's ranch. He knew everyone. It was neutral ground and a commonality that she would have with only a few, but his passions didn't seem to lie within the boundary lines of the guest ranch. Rather, they seemed to be following his heart all around the world—living for adventure. He seemed like the kind of guy who was far more at home jumping out of an airplane than sweeping a floor.

He lived for his dreams.

She closed her eyes and leaned her head against the window. If only she had the same freedoms.

There had been a brief period of time, right after she had moved out of her mother's house after her parents' divorce, when she could have escaped. She could have gone anywhere in the world. At the time, she'd barely had two dimes to her name, but if she had truly wanted to get out, she could have. There was nothing holding her back—except her own fears and feelings of inadequacy. She hadn't wanted to travel the world alone. Adventures alone were nothing compared to adventures with someone you loved—and that feeling had led her straight to her sister, and the gates of Dunrovin.

Until now, she hadn't looked back. Yet, sitting next to Waylon—a man who was living his dreams—Christina couldn't help but feel like she had missed a chance of a lifetime. Now she couldn't go—she had to think of Winnie. She had to think of her life at the ranch. Family, and the ability to support them, came first.

The truck slowed down, and they bumped up the driveway leading to the Poes'—or rather William Poe's—house. She still hadn't gotten over her friend's death. Every time she thought of Monica, she had to remind herself that she was gone. It was surreal. So many times over the last few days, she had lifted her phone to text her friend, only to remember that she was gone.

Though everything had changed in her world, the Poes' house hadn't. The siding was the same gray it had been a few months ago, and the garage stood apart from the house, filled with William's collection of cars, its walls adorned with *Sports Illustrated* posters of scantily clad women.

She'd never liked stepping foot in the garage, and she had liked William even less—especially after Monica had told her about his private habits, which mostly centered on getting himself between the legs of as many women as humanly possible. How Monica had put up with it was still a mystery to her, but she'd always supported her friend. It wasn't her place to judge her, but only to stand by her side.

Monica's car was parked outside, like now that she was dead, there wasn't a place in William's home for any of his wife's leftovers.

"You okay?" Waylon asked as she noticed him glancing over at her.

"Yeah, I'm fine. I've just made it a habit over the years not to hang out here. Monica was good about it—she normally let me meet her somewhere else."

"You were friends with Monica? The lady your sister…" He stopped, like he was afraid that the words *your sister killed* would break her once again.

She couldn't deny the fact he might have been right in his assumption. Even the thought of what her sister had done to her friend, and her reasons behind it, made a feeling of sickness rise up from her belly.

"Yeah. Monica is a cool—I mean, *was* a cool chick. She loved to ride horses. We'd spend hours riding the trails around the ranch. Honestly, looking back, I think it was just an excuse for her not to be around her husband."

Waylon chuckled. "It's funny how hindsight is always twenty-twenty."

"Is that how you feel when you look back at your marriage with my sister?"

His face pinched slightly at the question, like he wished she hadn't gone there. Lucky for him, as they pulled to a stop in front of William's house, the man in question came out the door. William grimaced as he caught sight of them, and Christina would have sworn she could see him mouth a long line of curse words.

Instead of answering her question, Waylon jumped out of the truck like he would rather face the cussing county tax appraiser than talk any more about his failed marriage.

She couldn't blame him. Relationships, and what came of them, were a tricky thing—especially in their case. Even as she thought about their confusing circumstances, she couldn't help but watch as Waylon strode toward William.

His jeans had to have been made especially for him. There was no way something that fit that well around the curves of his ass could have simply come off a rack.

She giggled as she thought about the many

web articles she had read about men who didn't wash their jeans so they could get them to fit that way. Was Waylon among the no-wash crew? It was a random thought, but in a way it made her like him even more. It was almost as if the thought of him standing over his jeans at night and deciding whether or not they should be cleaned made him more human and less the imposing MP who had literally landed on her doorstep. More than anything, it made him real. Human. Attainable. But was he someone she really wanted to be with?

Waylon turned around and waved for her to come out of the truck.

She'd much rather have stayed—she had nothing to say to William Poe that she hadn't already said. They'd had their moment together at Monica's funeral. He had barely spoken to her or looked at her as they had stood at the cemetery, watching as people threw handfuls of dirt onto his wife's casket. Yet, afterward, when everyone was saying their goodbyes, he'd made his position clear when he'd leaned in and said a few simple but inflammatory words: "This is all your fault."

At the time, she hadn't understood his thought process. How could he have possibly thought she had anything to do with his wife's death? Sure, she had ties to all involved, but that didn't mean she had taken a role in anything. On the other hand, she wasn't completely innocent—there had been the night in the office when she had been talking about William and his actions with Monica. Alli had been just outside the door, listening to their conversation. No doubt that night she had drawn her sister's crosshairs onto Monica's back, but William couldn't have known.

He was just angry, and she had been his easiest and closest target. Maybe because he couldn't go after her sister, he had simply decided to come after her. Regardless, she hated him and how his choices had been an atomic bomb in all of their lives. If he had just kept himself in his pants, lives could have been saved and Alli would have never disappeared. He was like this town's Helen of Troy, but instead of his face launching a thousand ships, his manhood had launched a thousand hours of tragedy.

She clomped out of the truck and made her way over to the two men. William gave her the same look of disgust he had given her at Monica's funeral, like he had bitten into a wormy apple. The only worm here was him.

"I believe I answered all the questions when your brother brought me in, Waylon." As William spoke, a small dark-haired woman walked out of the house. William, noticing the woman, turned and pointed toward the door. "Get back inside, Lisa."

"Why are *they* here?" The woman pointed toward her with a shaking finger. "Did they find Alli?"

"Shut up and listen to me, Lisa. Go inside."

Lisa looked taken aback, but she hurried inside.

"Who was that?" Christina asked.

William waved her off. "*She* is none of your business."

Was the woman just another in his long line of conquests?

"You people have no right to be stepping on my property, and you have no right to be asking me any questions," William continued.

"You're right. You're under no real obligation. Nothing you tell me would be admissible in court," Waylon said, in an almost jovial tone, as if he could win the slimeball's favor by acting like a friend. "However, I would think you would want to bring your wife's murderer to justice."

"You don't want justice," William said with a snort. "You just want to find Alli. You think if you can get to her first, maybe you can get her a lighter sentence when the crap rains down. But here's the deal..." William pointed at Waylon, the move aggressive and escalating. It was the move of a politician. "*Even if* you find her, she's going to pay for what she did. She'll get the full weight of justice upon her. I will make sure of it."

"*Even if?* What, do you think there's a chance we aren't going to find my sister?" Christina asked, enraged by the man's tone. "What did you do to her?"

"Better yet," Waylon interrupted, "what didn't you tell my brother about what you know?"

William waved them off. "You and your

screwed-up family aren't my problem. You people are trash." He looked into her eyes. "*You* are trash. And if you think I'm going to play your effing games, you're wrong."

"*Our* games?" Waylon looked genuinely confused by the man's accusation. "What games are you talking about, Will?"

"My name's William, not Will, Bill or Billy. Unlike you, Waylon, I wasn't named after a dead country singer. My family wasn't a bunch of rednecks."

Up until that point, Christina had thought she had the corner on hating William Poe. Yet, based on the flaming-red color of Waylon's face, she might have just lost the lead position.

"Listen here, bastard," Waylon seethed. "I would've liked to go about this whole thing amicably. You could have made this all easy."

"Who the hell do you think you are?" William interrupted him, making a thin sheet of sweat rise to Waylon's forehead as his hands balled into tight fists. "You came here. You're accusing me of who knows what. You have no right to be here—and the only bastard here is you."

Waylon lunged forward, but Christina stopped him by grabbing his hand. "Come on, Waylon." She pulled him toward the truck. "If nothing else, now you know the type of guy that would lead a woman to kill."

Chapter Five

Eloise had been cooking constantly since Waylon had stepped foot back onto the ranch, and the rich odors of roasting meat and butter wafted throughout the house. After their run-in with William, Christina was more than happy to settle back into the warmth and comfort of the kitchen as she helped Eloise put the finishing touches on the meal.

Waylon and Colter walked in, but they were so wrapped up in whatever they had been talking about that neither of them seemed to notice her sitting at the bar.

Colter looked a lot like his older, biological brother. They both had the same copper-tinted skin, dark brown eyes and jet-black hair, but beyond their looks, the two were nothing alike. Waylon carried himself as though he were ready to take on the world, while Colter...well, it could be said that he was constantly at ease. It was almost as if Waylon carried a chip on his shoulder big enough for the both of them, so big that Colter had never felt its weight.

"Heya, Colt," Christina said, giving him a small wave.

He smiled brightly, the simple action lighting up his face with his characteristic warmth. "How's it going, lady? Long time no see." He walked over and gave her a hug so big that her feet came off the floor.

She laughed, but she couldn't help but notice the frown that flickered over Waylon's features at his brother's display of affection. Or was it that his brother had suddenly displayed a bit of affection toward her? Either way, she pried herself out of Colt's arms.

Winnie came running into the kitchen. There was dirt streaked over her face, and her Ace bandage was covered in sticky greenish-brown mud.

"Winnie, were you out in the barn again?" Christina asked, giving the girl an admonishing look.

"Lewis and Clark gotta have cookies," Winnie said, like giving horses their treats was a vital part of any growing girl's day. "They so hungry."

Christina fell victim to the girl's big brown eyes—eyes that looked entirely too much like her father's. She instinctively glanced toward Waylon. He was smiling at the girl, and the warmth made her heart shift in her chest. He wasn't supposed to like children—especially

Winnie. If he fell for the girl's charms and the time came when he was given a choice of having her, Christina would undoubtedly lose out to him and the girl would be taken away.

She wrapped her arms around Winnie, claiming her even though Waylon had no idea she was up for grabs. "Why don't we go get you cleaned up before supper. Your—" She stopped before she let the word *nana* fall from her lips. She didn't want him to ask about the moniker again. The less he knew, the easier it would be.

"What?" Winnie looked up at her.

"Nothing. Let's just get you cleaned up. You don't want to be a mess when it comes time to eat."

Winnie pulled out of her arms. "You're gonna play dress up." She pointed toward Waylon. "Yeah, Way-lawn?"

His handsome and confusing smile disappeared. He might have liked Winnie, but he probably wasn't any closer to wanting a kid than at the moment he'd landed.

"Ah, yeah," he said, pulling the word into a long collection of syllables. "You still want to do that, eh?" He looked over toward Christina, sending her a questioning glance.

She shrugged. He could stay in the hot seat for a little while longer. Sometimes all it took for a man to go running was an hour with a mercurial toddler—especially his type, the kind who didn't know the difference between a sippy and a bottle.

Winnie ran over, took him by the hand and started to drag the begrudging Waylon toward her room at the far end of the ranch-style house. She and Alli had shared a room, but now she was on her own.

"Come on, Way-lawn. It's gonna be fun!" Glee filled Winnie's words, so much so that

Christina was tempted to let him off the hook and take his place.

She didn't mind living in the land of Pinterest costumes and childish dreams. She embraced country living—a world of quilting parties and Sunday dinners. She found great comfort in the fact that they had their own lifestyle and their own brand of perfection.

Even though Waylon had grown up in this world, the tight look on his face made it clear he didn't have the same sentimental attachment. He looked like he would be far more comfortable in the throes of war than the throes of pink felt and glitter.

Eloise walked out of the kitchen carrying a bag of frozen corn as Waylon made his way into the girl's room. "Is he really going to go with her?" she asked, her eyes wide with surprise.

"You know Winnie. She has a way of convincing even the stillest of hearts to start beating again."

Eloise gave her a soft, knowing smile. "I don't think it's just Winnie who has that gift."

She wasn't sure exactly what the woman was implying, but the thought made Christina shift her weight uncomfortably. She wasn't having any effect on Waylon, and whether or not Waylon was making her feel unexpected and somewhat unwelcome things...well, there was no way the woman could have known.

Before Eloise could make her think of anything else, she escaped down the hall after the keeper of hearts. She stood outside the bedroom door, listening to Winnie telling Waylon about her stuffed animals. Apparently, according to the story she was telling him, her favorite was her orange-and-white plush cat she had dubbed Mr. Puffy Face. Yesterday the cat had been dubbed Hank; regardless, their interaction made Christina laugh. Winnie hadn't been herself since her mother's disappearance, and it was nice to see some happiness return to the girl.

She leaned against the doorjamb, the door open just far enough to see in but not far enough to interrupt the two from their play. Winnie had put on her pink Sleeping Beauty dress, and Waylon had a purple bejeweled tiara perched at an awkward angle on his head.

Christina chuckled as she turned back to the kitchen.

Eloise pulled out the roast from the oven as Colter stirred the vegetables. From the formal dining room, she could hear the titters of laughter as Wyatt and his fiancée, Gwen, set the table. As she stood watching, a comforting feeling of home filled her.

It felt so good to be a part of all of this—and the family. If she had been on her own with

Alli's disappearance, she didn't know how she would have been able to make it this far—just taking care of Winnie was a full-time event, and that was to say nothing of her job at Dunrovin, taking care of the animals and helping to train the horses, and the daily needs of living. It felt so good, standing here and letting life go on around her.

It made her wish this moment could last forever—but bad or good, all things in life were dictated by the fickle hands of time. Even intangible things like love fell victim to it—love ebbed and waned, or at least it always had when it had come to the men in her life.

The only time that wasn't true was when it came to her love for Winnie. To love a child was an incredible experience. They could drive her to the edges of madness, they could treat her worse than a stranger, and yet at the end of the day, all their trespasses could be forgiven with the whisper of *I love you*, or their scent on her skin. Christina hugged her arms around herself as she thought about how close those days could be to coming to an end.

"Is Waylon going to make it out of that bedroom alive?" Wyatt asked, pulling her from the pits of her thoughts.

"I—" she started but was cut off as Waylon appeared in the kitchen's doorway, sadly without his sparkling tiara.

"Is there any tinfoil?" he asked, a childlike smile on his face.

Eloise opened up a drawer, pulled out a blue box and handed it over to Waylon. "You're not going to make her dress up like leftovers, are you? Winnie isn't going to go for the idea," she said with a chuckle.

He raised the box like a wand. "No worries, I have this under control."

"Is that army-speak for you are letting a two-

and-a-half-year-old run you?" Wyatt asked with a raise of his brow and a thin smirk.

Waylon laughed, and his whole face lit up. His copper skin made the crow's feet nearly invisible at the corners of his eyes, but if she looked closely, she could just make them out, almost as if they were a secret about him that was there only for her. She tried to control the drive she felt to move nearer to him, but as she stared, her desire intensified.

"Hey, now, I've let worse women control me. At least this one's cute, she likes me and she enjoys having me around—it's a lot more than I can say about some others," Waylon joked, but as he looked at Christina, he shut his mouth like he wished he could have reeled the words back in. "I...I just mean..." he stammered. "Not that I meant Alli or anything."

"I'm not going to say anything," she said, cutting him a little slack. "I have no room to judge anyone when it comes to relationships."

She could have sworn she saw Eloise and Gwen share a look. They were wrong if they thought something was happening between her and Waylon. There weren't any feelings between them—at least not any that came from Waylon—and her feelings were probably nothing more than her trying to come to terms with his new bond with Winnie. Regardless of whatever those two women were thinking, the only thing she and Waylon would share was the love they each felt toward one curly-haired two-year-old.

She turned away as Waylon brushed against her, making his way back to the girl. Where he had touched her burned with an unexpected and unwelcome heat, and she rubbed her arm as though she could make the feeling disappear by wiping it away.

The door to Winnie's room clicked shut, and Wyatt peeked around the corner before turning back to everyone in the kitchen. "Have you told him yet?"

She glanced down at the floor, afraid that if she looked at Wyatt he would be able to read each confusing thought and feeling that ran through her.

"Don't you think he has a right to know?" Wyatt pressed.

Eloise waved him off. "He has every right to know, but it's already been nearly three years. What's another few days?"

"He's going to be furious when you tell him. He's never going to understand. I know I wouldn't," Wyatt continued.

Gwen walked over to him and wrapped her arm around his. "This isn't our choice, Wyatt."

"That doesn't mean that we aren't going to be accountable when he learns the truth." Wyatt put his hand on his fiancée's and made small circles on the back of her skin.

The simple action made Christina want to hug herself tighter. Gwen was so lucky to have found love with one of the Fitz brothers. They all had their issues, but they were all good people, even Waylon—or rather, especially Waylon. She could only imagine how good it would feel to have him making small circles on her skin, especially after him merely brushing against her had almost brought her to her knees.

She forced herself to look away from the cute couple, reminding herself that as picturesque as they were, a relationship wasn't what she wanted. Sure, it started out with flowers, sweet words and tender touches, but nothing that good lasted forever.

"If we tell him," Eloise said, pulling her from her thoughts, "there will be no going back. Once the truth is out there, he's going to have to make some major choices in his life. He's innocent in all this. He has always done his best, and I'm sure if we tell him the truth, he will try to make the best choices he can. But who knows what those choices will be."

Wyatt shook his head. "We can't stand in his way."

"I know," Eloise said. "Right now, with all the uncertainty with Alli and what she may or may not do... Well, he's already burdened enough. Don't you think?"

"Give him more credit. He's strong. He can handle the truth. And he needs to be able to make his own decisions." Wyatt motioned toward the bedroom.

"No one is arguing that, Wyatt," Christina said, trying to come to Eloise's aid. "It's just that we need to make sure he's ready."

"Come on," Wyatt said, shaking his head. "No one's ever really ready to be a parent. Even if you think you are ready, it's not until you're thrown into the situation that you really know what you're in for."

Eloise smiled as she raised her brow. "Is there something you two need to tell us?" She rubbed a small circle on her lower belly.

Gwen's mouth dropped open. "No… I… Not yet…" she stammered.

Wyatt chuckled. "Mom, come on. Don't tease her."

Eloise laughed. "There's nothing wrong with me hoping for a few more grandchildren. It's never too soon to start trying." She gave them all a little wiggle of the finger. "Little Miss Winnie needs a partner in crime."

Gwen's face was bright red, and Wyatt had started to take on a sweaty sheen. Christina felt for them and the pressure the matron of the family was putting on them. At least she wasn't in their shoes. She might be asked about her relationship status all the time—it was the curse of being over twenty-three and not married—but those questions were far easier to field when compared to talk about babies.

Thankfully, before any more uncomfortable questions, the door to Winnie's room opened. They all went silent.

Waylon walked into the kitchen. He frowned. "What's going on? Why are you guys so quiet?"

Eloise smiled. "What, kiddo? We aren't being quiet. We were just waiting on you two rascals to be done playing around before we sit down to eat." She motioned to the roast, once again taking control of the situation like a master.

Christina smiled. She could learn a few things from Eloise.

"Okay." From the way Waylon stood there looking at his mother for a moment, it was easy to see he didn't believe her, but he didn't press them further. He shook his head and turned away from them toward the hall. "If you are all ready, I'm proud to present Princess Leonia of Leo Land and her cat, Mr. Puffy Face." He gave an over-the-top whirl of the hand and a deep, exaggerated bow.

He stood up and started to hum the theme song for the Miss America pageant. Christina couldn't help the laugh that escaped her. It was surreal to be watching the oh-so-handsome MP doing tongue trills for the entrance of a two-year-old.

Winnie marched into the kitchen. Her walk was more like the cowgirl she was instead of the princess she was pretending to be. She had on the pink Sleeping Beauty gown, her bandaged arm was wrapped with tinfoil to make it look like a clunky sword and she wore a foil crown. The crumpled and uneven crown had two large spikes Christina was sure were supposed to be purely decorative but looked conspicuously like devil horns.

Winnie had on bright pink lipstick that was smeared over her teeth as she smiled, and it was heavy on the left side of her mouth, like Waylon had pressed too hard while applying. Winnie smiled brightly, the motion filling her eyes with joy.

Oh, what it would have been to be a child once again, to find true, unadulterated joy in things most stodgy adults thought ridiculous. It would have been so nice to go back to those moments in life, where a thing like playing dress-up was all it took to forget one's troubles. There were no concerns of what was to come, bills that needed to be paid or the things that were required to make another person happy. There was just one pink dress and one ill-fitting tinfoil crown.

Wyatt leaned in close so only Christina could

hear him. "He isn't perfect, neither is his life, but maybe he wouldn't be such a bad dad after all."

He hadn't needed to tell her what she was already thinking. Some things—like the look of pride that Waylon was giving Winnie—spoke volumes about what it meant to truly love. And love was the only thing that really mattered.

Chapter Six

Waylon had never been one for sleep much, but last night had been long and filled with dark shadows. It was almost as if Dunrovin had started to move in around him, threatening to trap him with its candy canes and pink princesses. He had managed to escape once before, but it had been when things had been ending with Alli. Now that he was back at the ranch, it was hard to remember any of the other reasons he'd left besides his disastrous marriage.

Rolling out of bed and making his way to the kitchen, he was surprised to find Christina already standing in front of the coffeepot as it percolated and bubbled with life. The scent of hot coffee filled the kitchen, but beneath it was the heady aroma of the woman standing with her back to him. The strange mixture made him suck in a long breath, pulling the scent of her deep into his lungs. She smelled like shampoo, hay and something earthy. It reminded him of something he couldn't quite put his finger on.

Christina swayed her hips as though she were dancing to a song only she could hear, but as she moved, she hummed a few bars. A piece of hair fell from the butterfly clip that held up her blond locks. She was so dang beautiful. If he wasn't here about her sister, if he was just living his everyday and somewhat mundane life back at Fort Bragg, he would have made his move. As it was, he simply stood there, taking her in.

Last night there had been a moment when he'd been dancing with Winnie in her princess dress and he had caught Christina smiling. That look had almost made it seem possible she liked him, but he wasn't sure he was qualified to get a good read on that woman. She was so confusing. Mad one minute, and the next she was giving him a look that in most circles meant they would be exchanging more than phone numbers.

He chuckled.

Christina turned around with a jump. "How long have you been standing there?" She pulled at her Van Halen nightshirt. There was a hole over her left hip, and her hand found the spot like she hated the thought of him seeing any part of her naked flesh.

He smiled as he stared at her fingers and thought about the word *naked*. Just the thought made his body quiver to life. Yes, he could handle seeing her lying on his bed, waiting, wanting.

"Waylon, how long have you been there?" She

gave him a look as though she was wondering if he had lost his mind.

"Huh? Not long." He forced himself to look at the clock on the stove while he tried to get his body back under control, but mornings and him…well, it was just another battle that he rarely seemed to win. He shifted his weight to hide anything that might have slipped into view. "Actually, I was just going to grab a cup of joe before heading up to where they found Alli's car."

"I thought you might have something in mind. I'm glad I caught you. I want to go."

"Haven't you already gone up there?" A minute ticked by on the clock.

She turned back to the cupboard and took out two travel mugs. "Yep, but after I saw you work the investigation on the car yesterday… well, I would love to think that you might be able to pull something from the scene, just like you pulled that note out of the headliner."

That was pure dumb luck, but he wasn't sure he wanted to admit it to her. He liked the thought of her thinking he had some special gift when it came to an investigation. He would take being her hero any day.

"I doubt there's anything left up there for us to find. They went over that scene pretty good, according to Wyatt's notes. And it's been nearly a full week. By now, between the weather and normal wear and tear—well, we'd be lucky to even find the exact spot."

"I've been up there. I can show you where they found the car." Christina sloshed the coffee into the cups. Her hands were shaking slightly.

"Are you okay?" he asked, motioning toward her unsteady hands.

She set the coffeepot back in the maker and balled her fists, like she was mad at them for giving her weakness away. "I'm fine. Just fine." As she looked up at him, there was a faint redness to her cheeks.

He didn't push it. It would make all their lives easier if they could get along for the few days he was here, and he had a feeling that if he questioned her, things had the chance of slipping back into a place where she barely seemed to tolerate him.

"Here." She handed him one of the travel mugs. "You take it black, right? Every cop I know always takes their coffee black. I always thought it was some statement about being so tough that you all don't need cream and sugar, but when I asked Wyatt about it, he said it was that you all were just too lazy to put extra work into something that was good just plain." She was rambling, and as she spoke, the redness in her cheeks grew more pronounced and she was forced to put her hands around her own cup to keep them from shaking.

"Yep, I'm one who takes it black. But I got a buddy back at Bragg who loves so much cream that I always say it's just cream with a splash of coffee," he joked, trying to make her feel better. He took a sip of the steaming liquid.

The woman knew how to make a good cup of joe, and it made him wonder what else she was good at.

"Are you sure you're not going along just so you can spend more time with me?"

She gave him a cute smirk and a raise of her eyebrow. "It's about my sister. Not you and me."

"You and me?" he teased. "Don't you think you could just call that *us*?"

She took a long drink of her coffee. It was so long, in fact, he couldn't help but wonder how she wasn't burning her tongue.

"It's really all just semantics," he continued. "I'm not saying there is an us. Just that…"

She lowered her coffee, and there was a smile on her lips. "You can stop. We both know where each other stands—and it certainly isn't something that needs to be discussed." She refilled her cup. "By the way, when are you thinking you're going to head back to your base?"

"I have a week's leave. The only reason I got it at all is that my CO owed me a couple of favors. They don't like giving leave when a person only has a few months left before re-enlisting."

She frowned at him. "So you're going to go for another four years?"

He shrugged. "I only have about six months left this round. I love my job and my buddies in my unit. We are like family."

"*Like* family," she said, repeating his words as though she was trying them on for size. "Is your job pretty dangerous?" She looked up at him, and there was something in her eyes that made him glance away out of fear that she would be able to see into his memories.

There was always danger in his job. Each day was something different. The last major incident had been when he had stepped in the way of a sniper's bullet in Fallujah for his CO. Luckily, the bullet had mostly impacted Waylon's Kevlar, but a small fragment had managed to break loose and hit him in the elbow. From time to time, his left arm still pinged, reminding him of how close he could have been to losing his life for the greater good. Yet, from the look on Christina's face, the last thing he needed to do was admit that he was always toeing a thin line between life and death.

"Let's go," he said. "And no more questions."

Her frown deepened. "Look, if you don't want me to go…"

"You'd stay here?" he asked with a playful smile. "We both know you aren't the type who is going to sit by and idly twiddle her thumbs. No matter what you think of me, you won't miss this chance."

"Let me go get dressed," she said, setting down her coffee. "Don't go anywhere." She gave him a threatening look.

Waylon raised his hands in surrender. "Cross my heart."

She rushed out of the room and he could hear her run down the hallway. A couple of minutes later she returned, cowgirled out—complete with a pair of ostrich-skin boots, a tight-fitting pair of jeans, and a purple plaid shirt. She had her coat draped over her arm.

"You ready to go?"

"Always."

He walked to the car, holding the door as she followed.

Each time she drew close to him, he couldn't help his need to pull her scent deep into his lungs. Dang, she smelled so good.

They drove in silence, passing through the gates of the mountains that led to the Montana/ Alberta border. He hadn't made this drive in a long time, and as they passed by the crystal-blue lakes and clear rivers, he just took it all in. This place was so beautiful. It really was the Last Best Place, just as its slogan said. There was something about Montana that beckoned to days gone by, of the untamed nature of life and the ones who dared live it.

"I'm sorry about yesterday. When you flew in. It was just…with Winnie and all…I guess… Just know that I don't hate you or anything. Sometimes I can just be a little prickly," Christina said, breaking the silence between them.

She sounded sincere enough, but he wasn't sure he entirely bought what she was trying to sell. "Honestly, I get it—I mean, if you hate me or whatever. Divorce leads to division among friends and even more among families. You have your sister's back, and I admire that kind of loyalty—even if it's to my disadvantage."

She stared at him for a moment, like she was surprised by his candor, but she didn't say anything.

"My family had their fair share of dislike when it came to your sister. It would only be right that you would have the same feelings toward me. But I want you to know that, regardless of what Alli told you, there was a lot more to the situation. I doubt she told you everything that led up to our divorce." He gripped his hands tight on the steering wheel of her truck. "I mean, I wasn't without guilt. I certainly made my fair share of mistakes, but I wasn't the only one who made some bad choices."

She glanced down at her hands. "I know I

only got one side of the story. I've come to realize that, thanks to you being here. I can see the way you are with your family and how you're trying with Winnie. You don't need to worry about my opinion. Besides, I heard something the other day that kind of put things into perspective for me, and I know it's as true for me as it probably is for you."

"What did you hear?"

She looked up at him and sent him a soft smile that made his stomach flip.

"They said that everyone's life is a book, and in each book there is one chapter no one is willing to read aloud."

He chuckled. "Just one chapter?"

Her smile widened. "Hey, it's just what they said." She shrugged.

For a moment, he considered reaching over and taking her hand, but he couldn't bring himself to do it. They had finally started to move together. He would hate to screw it up by taking things in a direction that she had no intention of going. For now, he would have to be happy with just seeing her smile and ignore the way his body seemed to want to pull him closer to her.

"The spot was right up there," Christina said, pointing to a nondescript little pullout on the side of the nearly deserted highway.

There were tall dead grasses on the side of the road, and down the embankment was a pond and a meadow that brushed against the toes of the mountains that stood like sentinels around the valley. Snow had started to accumulate on the peaks of the range, a visible reminder that icy storms lurked just over the horizon.

He parked the truck, and they got out as a big rig barreled down the road past them. It made the air shudder as the driver changed speeds, the sound almost deafening.

"Where do you think he's coming from?" Waylon asked, motioning toward the truck as it rumbled north.

"Truckers use this highway when the weather is good. It's a bit longer in mileage than the main highway, but they make up for it in speed. It can cut up to an hour off their transit to the border. The people who live along here hate it. Two years ago, a big rig carrying crude oil overturned. Ruined their groundwater. The EPA had to come in and do all kinds of studies. They finally cleared the area for general use again, but if you ask anyone who actually lives around here, there is still oil that seeps through the ground and into their water."

He would have asked how the oil company had gotten away with dodging responsibility, but he knew all too well how the feds liked to work. He'd been living in their world for too long to be oblivious to the fact that they often were willing to accept a little bit of collateral damage when millions of dollars were at stake.

"There are a few locals who like the truckers, though," Christina continued.

"Who's that?"

She motioned down the road. "There is a small town about fifteen miles from here that pretty much only exists thanks to the long-haul trade. It's the last stop for gas and grub before the truckers head over the border."

His mind went to the receipt Wyatt said he'd found in Alli's car. He'd said it was of no use, but maybe it was from the town Christina was talking about. It could have been more of a clue than his brother had realized, but what did it really matter if Alli had stopped for gas in the little town before heading over the border, or had she come back sometime later in the day? It would be a normal thing to do. Wyatt had said he'd looked into the lead. If it had been anything, his brother would have figured it out. He was a good cop and an even better brother.

Waylon walked to the edge of the pullout. No matter how badly he wanted to find something definitive that could point them in Alli's direction, there was nothing besides gravel on the side of the road. He stood there for a moment, taking in the mountains and the aroma of winter. The cold air bit at his nose, sharp and clean—a far cry from the dry and dusty air of Iraq.

"You okay?" Christina asked, stepping beside him. "You're being quiet."

"Just thinking," he said, looking over at her. His gaze moved down to her hands. Her fingers looked so inviting. He could almost feel them slipping between his, and the sensation made his hand twitch.

"About?" she pressed.

He couldn't tell her that he was really thinking about how badly he wanted to touch her, and how she reminded him of how lonely his life had been ever since he'd left Montana and Alli. Maybe that was all his desire to touch her was—a need to stave off the loneliness. No, that probably wasn't it. He'd had plenty of chances to be with other women, and none of them had made him give even a passing thought to anything resembling a relationship. Yet something about Christina and the way she pushed him made him wonder if he'd made a mistake in leaving Mystery. But if he'd stayed, there was no way they would have ended up together, either.

Oh, Alli. When they found her, she would never let him and Christina be together. She would do and say everything she could to stop her sister from being with him.

Everything about him and Christina and the attraction he felt wasn't going to work—a relationship with her wasn't just unlikely, it was almost forbidden.

As much as he wished the thought would push him away from her, it only made him want her that much more.

If he was going to have a chance with Christina, he had to make things happen before Alli came back into their lives and had the chance to screw everything up.

He reached over and took Christina's hand. Alli had already messed up enough in his life— he wouldn't let her stand in the way of him following his heart. Christina jerked as their skin touched, but she didn't pull away. Rather, she moved her fingers between his and drew him closer.

His heart leaped into his throat. Maybe he wasn't alone in his desire.

There was the rumble of another big rig, but this time the roar seemed deeper and the rig slowed down, pulling to a stop behind their truck. He frowned in the trucker's direction. He'd finally made his move with Christina and the dude was ruining it.

She pulled her fingers from his and moved a few steps away from him, almost as if she regretted her decision to let him touch her.

"Heya," the trucker said as he stepped down from the cab. His hair was long and unkempt, and as he looked at them, he ran his fingers through the greasy mess. "You guys need help?" he asked, his voice flecked with a Canadian accent even though his rig had Montana plates.

Waylon had forgotten about Montana and its unspoken pay-it-forward code. If someone was broken down on the side of a road like this, there was always someone willing to help. The system came from the days of the pioneers. Not much had changed from those days, because in the dead of winter, in a place like this, it might be hours—if not days—before a person ran into someone else. In such a barren world, a single act of kindness could sometimes be the difference between life and death.

"We're good," Waylon said, trying his best to make himself smile at the well-intentioned interloper.

The trucker didn't stop; instead, he turned to Christina. "Are you okay, miss?"

Christina's eyes widened with surprise at the man's implied assumption that she might be here against her will. "I'm…I'm fine. Thanks for asking."

The guy dropped his hand. Until now Waylon hadn't noticed he was hiding a bat behind his leg.

Did this guy really think he was the kind of guy who would bring a girl out here to the middle of nowhere against her will? Or had the guy been around the world enough to jump to that kind of conclusion?

In a strange way, he was glad there were still guys out there like this trucker, men who were willing to come to the aid of a woman they didn't know. It gave him a little bit of hope for mankind.

"Army?" the trucker asked, motioning toward him.

"Huh?" Waylon glanced down at his clothes, half expecting to see his ACUs, but he was wearing jeans and a red plaid shirt. "Hoo-ah."

"I could tell from the look of ya. I can't believe they let you out of the desert playground."

"Ha," Waylon answered with a dry laugh. "Let me guess, you're a jarhead?"

"Some of us were born to be real men." The guy laughed, the sound high and tight.

Christina glanced over at him, like she was

trying to figure out what she was supposed to be doing while they chided each other.

"Sorry," Waylon said, motioning toward her. "This is my…" Dang, what did he call her? His former sister-in-law, his friend or his girlfriend? "This is my *friend* Christina. And, buddy, you are?"

The guy shook her hand. "I'm Daryl, Daryl Bucket," the man said, his voice flecked with a Canadian accent.

"Nice to meet you, Daryl," Christina said. "Thanks for stopping. That was noble of you. Let's chalk one up for the marines." She gave Waylon a teasing glance.

"Hey, now, you can't really give him a point. I traveled all the way across the country for this." He laughed.

She smiled, giving him a soft look that made it clear she was just joking around.

He turned to Daryl. "But really, that was

something, man. It's been a long time since I've been home. I forgot how selfless people around here can be."

"It ain't no thing." Daryl waved them off. "About a week ago I ran across a girl around here who was down on her luck. This is a hell of a spot for bad things to happen."

"You found a girl here a week ago?" All of Waylon's MP senses kicked into high gear. "What did she look like?"

The guy shrugged. "Average height, kind of skinny, dark haired. Nice enough lady."

"Did you catch her name?"

Daryl frowned as though he were trying to pull the name from somewhere deep in his thoughts. "Can't say that I did. I don't recall her giving it, though I think I asked."

The woman's description vaguely matched Alli's. Was it possible this guy had some connection to her?

"She was pulled over right here," Daryl continued, motioning toward the small pullout.

"Do you remember what kind of car she was driving?"

Daryl nodded. "Oh, yeah, it was a black Hyundai. Couple of years old. My ex-wife bought one just like it right before she and I split."

Waylon tried to play it cool, but his mind was buzzing.

"Did the lady tell you why she was pulled over?"

Daryl scratched his head. "She said she had a flat tire. I offered to change it for her, but she said she didn't have a spare and told me not to bother. Instead, she asked if I would give her a ride."

"To Canada?" Christina asked.

Daryl shook his head. "Nah, she wanted to go to some little town a ways south."

"Remember the town?"

"Of course I do, I live there. Moved to the place just after my divorce," Daryl said with a nod. "Lucky for her I was headed back home."

"Where do you call home?" Waylon pressed.

"It's a place called Mystery. You know it?"

Waylon looked over at Christina, and she gave him the nod that said she was thinking the same thing he was—they had just found the break they needed. They were one step closer to finding Alli, one step closer to going back to a life where the last thing they could have would be each other.

He stared at her blue eyes, taking them in like it was the last time he would really be able to look at her. She'd never be his, no matter how much he hoped for things to be different.

Chapter Seven

At least there was some kind of good news. Finally. Her sister was alive. Or at least Alli had been alive when Daryl had found her. Only the fates knew if she was still alive and kicking, or what was going on in her mind, but for the first time in a week, the sick feeling in Christina's stomach lessened.

Though when the trucker had told them he'd taken Alli back to Mystery, she wasn't sure if she was furious or relieved. How could her sister have run away only to come back the same day? She must have been running purely for show, but why? Why had she come back to town? Moreover, had she been watching them at the ranch?

There had been so many whispers about her sister still being a danger to the residents of the ranch and the town, but until now Christina had brushed them aside. Alli had wanted to kill Bianca and Monica because they had stood in the way of her relationship with William, but that didn't make her a threat to the rest of the population.

But maybe she had her sister all wrong. Maybe Alli was far more dangerous than she had assumed. Maybe Alli really had lost her mind like some people thought. Maybe she really did want to go on some kind of murderous rampage—or perhaps she had some kind of hit list. It was impossible to know until they found her.

Even though it was her sister, the thought

of Alli lurking in the shadows as she waited to take her next victim made Christina's skin crawl. Alli had been having so many issues, most circulating around her tumultuous relationships with men, and most recently William Poe. Maybe that was why she had come back— to watch William. Or was it possible she had something else in mind for the man, something more sinister?

Alli had always been the kind to hold a grudge.

Even though Christina hated the guy, she wasn't sure she could resist the urge to tell William that his life might be in danger. He had a right to know. She tried to tell herself it was unlikely, but with how strangely Alli had been acting before her disappearance, it was hard to tell what exactly her sister was thinking.

Christina sighed, watching the road as she and Waylon drove back toward the ranch.

"It'll all be okay." Waylon rested his hand palm up on the bench seat, waiting for her to slip her hand into his.

She stared at his fingers. With everything going on with Daryl, she had nearly forgotten about their moment, yet as she recalled the feeling of her hand in his, a warmth rose up from her core. There had been something so right about the feel of their entwined fingers.

In the still of the Montana roadside, she had even been able to feel his heartbeat, fast and erratic, as though he had been as anxious as she was. He was a beautiful specimen of a man. She had never thought of herself as ugly or unworthy, but there was no reason he should be nervous around her, a woman with no game and even less sexual acumen.

"I hope everything will be okay. I hope we can find her," she said, almost unaware of her words as she moved her trembling hand ever so slowly toward his waiting fingers.

It was funny how when she didn't have time to think about their actions, she had taken his hand and just lived in the moment. It had been unquestionably right to stand there, holding him. Yet, now that there was a chance to think of all the things that stood in their way, and all the reasons that they shouldn't be together, she wasn't sure that letting the wants of her body overrule the needs of her life was the right choice.

If they became anything more than acquaintances, she could only imagine what the rumor mill of Mystery would have to say. She wasn't a person who was overly consumed by what others thought or her image, but even a simple act like going to the grocery store would be met with whispers and poorly masked jabs at their choice to be together, as he had once been her sister's husband.

She could just have him for a few days. No one would have to know what went on between them—that was, as long as she could keep her head and her heart separate. She could enjoy his sexy body without the weight of worrying about the future. She'd never done the whole one-night-stand thing, but at her age it didn't seem like such a taboo. Perhaps she could even be empowered by living in a world where she could have sex just to have sex.

Throughout her life, her heart had only gotten in the way. This time she could just ignore it.

She smiled as she moved the last few inches and slipped her fingers between his.

It already felt good to do a little living.

Waylon squeezed her fingers. The action was small, but it ran through her entire being.

"I…" She wasn't sure of what to say, or if she

should tell him that she wanted this to be a no-strings type of thing.

"Alli is going to be all right. Now that we know she's alive, I'm sure we will find her," he said, going down an entirely different line of thinking.

She considered moving the conversation back to what she needed to say, but she stopped herself. It was better just to leave some things unspoken. Maybe that was what Waylon was thinking, too. He had to understand anything that came to be between them had a limited shelf life.

"Wait." She paused, letting what he'd said sink in. "You thought she was dead?"

Waylon's fingers tightened for a moment. "Well, she hasn't been seen in a week and no one has heard from her. You would have thought, with all the police and law enforcement involvement, if she was out there somewhere, someone would have at least reported seeing her by now. The only tips Wyatt has gotten so far are from a few folks who also reported seeing Elvis at the grocery store."

Alli couldn't be dead. Oh, the thought had crossed her mind. She just hadn't given it any room to grow. It just wasn't possible. Sure, some people would call her refusal to think about the possibility denial, but Alli being dead didn't even make logical sense—who would have wanted to kill her? Bianca's family hadn't taken the news of her death and Alli's involvement well, especially her mother, Carla, but not even she seemed like the type who would try to murder out of revenge or anger.

No. Alli had to be alive.

"She just dropped her car," Christina argued. "She didn't want anyone to find her. Really, it was smart."

"Sure," Waylon said with a slight nod. "It was

smart. She could travel with truckers, get lost in a sea of faces as she moved around the states. But there are a couple of things wrong with the idea. First, if she was going to drop her car and come back to Mystery, why would she have stopped at the little gas station and purchased enough gas to keep going for hours? And I'm still not sure how and if the note and the bullet we found are related."

He was right. It didn't make sense. "Maybe she wrote the note before everything fell apart and someone shot out the tire after she left the car. Who knows?" Christina said, trying to quell the fears that were rising within her about Alli's well-being.

"You're right, I don't understand your sister. And I really don't understand why she would have run away only to come back to Mystery."

"Maybe she just couldn't leave—" She stopped before she said Winnie's name aloud.

"I think we need to get back to Mystery, fast." Her thoughts raced to Winnie and the possible implications Alli's return to the town could have on the child's safety.

"Why?" he asked, pressing down hard on the accelerator without waiting for her answer. "What are you thinking?"

She shook her head. She had to tell him. If she did, maybe he wouldn't question things too much. And even if he did, she didn't have to answer him.

"Winnie... Winnie is Alli's daughter. I think she may be coming back to get her."

"Wait. She's *Alli's* daughter?" He jerked his foot off the gas pedal and stared over at her. "What? She couldn't get pregnant."

The way he said *pregnant* made it sound like some kind of expletive.

"She could and she did. And if Alli's come back, it's probably for Winnie."

He turned away from her and stared out toward the road as he stepped back on the gas. He sat in silence for a moment, just as she had feared he would. "So, how old is Winnie?"

Christina considered lying for a brief moment, but nothing good would come from it. "She's two."

His fingers moved on the wheel as though he were counting backward on them. He shook his head and gave a sigh of relief that made the knot that she didn't know was in her stomach loosen.

"She's two...so who's the father?"

Several of her own brand of expletives rolled through Christina's mind.

"I... She... You know Alli," she said, her voice as weak as her resolve. She should tell him. Now. He had asked her point-blank.

"She'd been seeing Poe, right?" Waylon asked. "You think he could be the girl's father?"

"No. She had Winnie before she started sleeping with him."

She hated being in this position. She hated this, but it wasn't just her choice to make to tell him. She and Eloise had agreed it would be better to break the news when everyone was there. If she let it slip now, Waylon would be so angry, and his mother wouldn't be there to defend herself. She had to protect Eloise by keeping the secret a little bit longer—Eloise was the closest person she had to a mother. It was only because of her that she wasn't living in some dank apartment on the wrong side of the tracks. She owed her everything—and that included her loyalty.

Yet that didn't mean she felt good about omitting the truth.

There was no right answer. There was only here and now, and what needed to happen.

"If Alli gets her hands on her daughter, we'll

never see her again. We need to keep Winnie safe. She needs to be protected."

"If Alli was going to take her, why would she have waited this long?"

He made a good point. "We really haven't left her alone. Someone is always with her."

"Even at night?" he asked with a raise of the brow.

Christina looked down at her hands. "Winnie has been sleeping with me ever since her mother disappeared. She's been having some abandonment issues and hasn't let us out of her sight."

"Oh, I see," he said as though he was suddenly reminded that Winnie was just a child, with childish needs. As Mystery came into view, he took in a long breath. "Do you really think Winnie's in danger? If she is, maybe it's best if I take care of her."

"You?" She didn't mean it to come out like

it did, with an air of shock and revulsion, but there was no taking it back.

From the look on Waylon's face, he was surprised and far more annoyed than she had intended for him to be.

"I just mean you have a lot on your plate already. The last thing you need while you're here is to have to take care of a child. The best thing you can do to keep Winnie out of Alli's hands is to make sure that you find her before she gets a chance to do something unspeakable." She paused. "Besides, Winnie is safe at the ranch."

He glanced over at her. "First, that's the first place Alli's going to come looking for the girl when and if she comes to get her. So we can't leave her there. Second, Alli may not even know I'm here. That gives us a little bit of an advantage when it comes to keeping the girl safe. She won't look for her with me. And third, I don't know who you think I am, but I swear

I'm not some monster with kids. I like kids. Just because I don't have any doesn't mean I'm completely inexperienced. Remember, I was in foster care for a long time. And when I was growing up, my mom and dad regularly took in foster kids that I helped care for."

"Having your own kids, or the sole care of a child, is totally different. You aren't ready." Her voice cracked like a whip, and she wished for a second time that she had better control of her tone.

He sucked in his breath. "You're right," he said, giving her an assessing glance. "I know it's different. And I know by what you are saying, and by the way you are saying it, it's probably coming from a place of deep hurt and pain—I know about your parents—but you can trust me."

"We can't fight about this. We just need

to find Winnie. She can go with Wyatt and Gwen," Christina said, not giving an inch.

She could trust a lot of things—the sun dawned in the east, the wind blew and time would always pass—yet she hadn't ever trusted a man. Not really. She wasn't about to start now, not when her niece's life could possibly be hanging in the balance.

Chapter Eight

She wasn't telling him something. Waylon could see it in the way she wouldn't look him in the eyes. He didn't know what she was holding back, but one thing he did know was that she was in full panic about Winnie. There was something about that little girl and Christina's concern for her safety that he couldn't ignore—or question.

She would tell him the truth if and when she was ready. He would just have to be patient.

His thoughts drifted to Winnie. The girl was two. He had divorced Alli three and a half years ago. That put Winnie well outside the range of the possibility of him being the father. At least, probably.

He tried to recall the last time he'd had relations with Alli, but all he could remember were times while they had still been married. He hated to think about that time in his life too much. Thoughts of what had transpired with Alli only brought heartache.

Wyatt and Gwen were in the barn with Winnie when they got back to Dunrovin.

Everything about the ranch was the same—the same weathered red barn and green stock fence around the corrals, the same red and green Christmas lights strung up around the barn, and the same American flag on the flagpole in the middle of the main house's front yard. It waved reverently, for a minute reminding him of what and whom he'd pledged his life to and why.

He followed Christina into the barn, watching her hips move and the Wranglers she was wearing stretch over the round curves of her ass. Her long blond hair fell down her back like a lion's mane, perfectly matching her proclivity for roaring. He didn't know a lot about astrological signs, but if he had to guess, she was probably a Leo.

As much as she drove him crazy, it was those same qualities—the tendency to push him away, to keep him guessing and to make the whole room turn with her smile—that made him want her more. She challenged him like no other woman ever had, and it was that mystery, that need to learn more, that made him wonder what it would be like to move back to the ranch—make a go of it here for a while.

He had planned on reenlisting, but now he wasn't so sure.

"Hey, guys!" Gwen said, looking up from the

horse she and Winnie were brushing. "How's it going?"

Winnie ran up to Christina and threw herself around her aunt's legs. As he watched, he recalled how Christina had told him she was merely the girl's guardian. Why had she been so evasive? She had said the father wasn't William and it wasn't him, so who could it be? And why wouldn't she just tell him?

Winnie let go of Christina and wrapped herself around his legs, then squirmed her way up, using her bandaged arm like a lever to move herself higher until she was snuggled into his arms. "Wy-ant said I can't wear my crown," she said in her slightly garbled toddler tongue. She pointed to her head.

"Why not?" Waylon said, pulling her higher into his arms so she could perch on his hip like a little bird.

She shrugged and popped her dirty thumb in her mouth.

"Weren't you just brushing the horses, kid?" he asked.

She smiled, not letting her thumb out of the cage of her teeth. "Yep. It was so funny. Lewis was being naughty." She nodded toward the bay gelding as he shifted his weight from one side to the other.

"I can't believe you wouldn't let her wear the crown we made. You're such a killjoy, man," he said to Wyatt with a laugh.

"Hey, now, little Miss Winnie, you know Lewis doesn't like shiny things. It spooks him. We don't want to scare him with your devil horns, do we?"

"Devil horns?" Winnie said with an overly exaggerated frown.

"Oh, I mean your *beautiful* crown." Wyatt laughed and pointed at his brother. "He may be good at a lot of things, but your buddy Waylon shouldn't be put in charge of costumes."

Winnie's frown deepened. "I looked bee-u-tiful."

"Of course you did, sweetheart," Gwen said, walking over and pulling the girl out of Waylon's arms. "Why don't you and I go have a little chocolate milk. Sound good?" She gave Wyatt a knowing look as she set Winnie down, and the girl took off toward the house without answering.

"Thanks, Gwen," Wyatt said, giving his fiancée a quick smack on the rear end.

"You need to put Lewis away, okay?" she said.

Wyatt nodded with a smile. The way he looked at Gwen made something shift in Waylon's chest. He couldn't recall ever looking at Alli the way Wyatt looked at Gwen.

He glanced over at Christina. Maybe there

would be a chance he could love someone the same way Wyatt and Gwen loved each other—like it was from the deepest part of their souls.

Wyatt unclipped Lewis's rope from the wall and led the horse back to his stall. The horse nickered as Wyatt closed the door. Wyatt walked over to the bucket, took out a few pellets and fed them to the gelding.

"So..." Wyatt said, "how'd it go up north? Did you guys find anything?"

Christina gave Waylon an uncomfortable glance and then her gaze fell to the floor.

"Actually, we ran into a trucker," Waylon said, telling him about Daryl Bucket and the ride to Mystery that he'd given Alli.

Wyatt's face tightened with anger as Waylon spoke.

"Why the hell would she come back here?" Wyatt asked, but as he looked over at Christina, he shut his mouth tight, like he'd suddenly answered his own question. "Winnie?"

"He knows she's Alli's daughter," Christina said, but her face was tight. "I think she's going to try to kidnap her."

"She wouldn't come back here for Winnie. That can't be it," Wyatt said, shaking his head in disbelief.

"There's no other reason, at least no good one, for her to be here," Waylon said. "We were thinking it would be best if we kept Winnie out of sight for a little while, at least until we have Alli in custody."

"I'll let Gwen know, and I'll stay with Winnie nonstop until we have Alli behind bars," Wyatt said. "Alli can't get an opportunity to get her hands on Winnie. If she does, I hate to think that Winnie's life would be in danger, but the truth is, I just don't know. All I know for sure is that if you give people the right motivations, they are capable of just about anything."

Waylon couldn't agree with his brother more. They couldn't trust his ex. The only people they could trust right now were family. No one could protect the little girl better than the people who loved her the most.

"I don't think Alli would hurt Winnie," Christina said, coming to her sister's defense.

"Are you really willing to put Winnie's life at risk just because you don't *think* your sister would do something sinister?" Wyatt asked.

"You were the one who suggested Winnie stay with Wyatt," Waylon said, arguing his brother's point.

Christina's eyes filled with tears. "It's just… I never thought Alli would do something like this."

"Don't worry, Christina. Gwen and I will take good care of our girl. In fact, I'll go grab them and we'll get out of here." Wyatt turned to Waylon. "Make sure to let Mom know we have Winnie when she gets back from the store, or she'll freak out."

"No problem," Waylon said as Wyatt rushed out of the barn.

Christina looked over at him, and he could sense her contempt. "My sister isn't as evil as you are both making her out to be."

He could understand why she was upset. If one of his brothers had done something like this, he would love them just as she loved Alli, and just like her, he would be stuck in a place between love of a person and hatred for their actions. Not for the first time since he'd met Christina, he wished he could pull her into his arms and heal her with his kiss.

NOTHING MADE SENSE. Her sister was out of control and acting in a way she never had before, and Christina had no idea what to think or do. She wished her sister would just turn herself in. Everything would be so much easier, and at least they would know she was out of harm's way.

Lately it seemed like wherever Alli was, trouble followed—and she was the source.

Christina sighed. Alli was trouble. There was no doubt about it, and as much as she loved her sister, she hated her equally.

She could feel Waylon looking at her. She glanced over at him and caught his eye. There was something in the way he looked at her that made her body come to life.

He smiled, and the sensation she was trying so hard to ignore boiled within her. No. It was nothing more than lust that she felt...tense, hungry, desperate lust. If she fell for that feeling, it would be far more dangerous than her sister. It would tear her world to pieces.

Then again, on the edges of lust was love. But falling in love with the man who promised nothing except his imminent departure was madness.

Danger and madness. It was the recipe for a disaster.

"Is there anywhere you think your sister would go?" Waylon asked, rescuing her from her thoughts.

She shook her head. "All she had was this ranch."

"Do you think it's possible that she went back to Poe? Would he shelter her from the police?"

"After what she did to Monica? No. Never. He hates her for what she did. He hates this entire ranch and everybody who works here and isn't afraid to tell everyone about it," Christina said. "Besides, Poe's already moved on to greener pastures."

"You're right. But if she's here in Mystery,

she has to be staying somewhere. Somewhere that no one would have noticed her."

The thought of someone hiding in the small town of Mystery was nearly laughable if it wasn't for the fact that, so far, Alli had been able to pull it off. There was no way she could go anywhere without someone knowing her, especially after the news of her role in Bianca's and Monica's deaths had hit the papers. She was unwelcome number one.

Even Christina had found herself getting the cold shoulder from some people within the community, especially those closest to Bianca. It was almost as if they blamed her for being the sister of a murderer—like in some way she could have stopped her sister from going mad.

Not for the first time, she wondered if she could have.

If she had just known more about her sister or if she had taken a more active role in her life,

maybe she could have stopped things from ever
going as far as they had.

She sighed. Whether or not the community
eventually forgot or forgave her—and the scar-
let letter she seemed to wear was removed—
her mistake in not being able to stop Alli was
something that would haunt her for the rest of
her life.

"Why don't we get out of here. Take a break."
Waylon reached over and took her hand. He
gave her fingers a light squeeze. "Sometimes
I find the answers I'm looking for in moments
when I'm not concentrating on the problem."

She knew exactly what he meant. She did that
all the time—for some reason, her best ideas
always seemed to come to her when she was in
the shower. Yet she wasn't about to say that to
Waylon. They weren't quite ready for a shower
or talk of one—at least not yet.

She blushed as she realized her thoughts had

devolved into her and Waylon making sweet, sweet love. It wasn't like she was a teenager who couldn't control herself, or who let her hormones drive her. She was a grown woman; she should have had far more restraint on her feelings.

That was what she was feeling—just some animalistic draw to the sexy Waylon Fitzgerald. Some primal instinct for sex. Simple procreative needs. Nothing more.

A strange calm filled her as she found a tendril of logic in her swarm of illogical feelings.

She let him lead her out as she stared at their knotted hands. Logic had to be her guide, not the feeling of heat that rose up from their melded touch or the happiness that threatened to overtake her at the mere fact he was touching her—moreover, that he *wanted* to touch her.

He must have had so many women interested in him. The thought made an unwelcome flutter of jealousy move through her. She looked up at his brown eyes and the almost imperceptible fine lines at their corners. He ran his thumb over her hand.

"What?" he asked, his voice raspy with something she recognized but refused to acknowledge even to herself.

"We've gone through all the guesthouses on the ranch from top to bottom." She tried to talk about something as distanced from feelings as possible. "Now that the main tourist season is over, we're buttoning up a few of them for the winter. And the rest we are keeping up and running for the fall guests and winter skiers." She knew she was rambling a bit, but he seemed to have a habit of making her do that.

His smile grew almost impossibly larger, as if he realized he was making her nervous. "Did she know the schedule of guests and which cabins you guys would be closing down for the season?"

"Everyone who works here would have had access to that information."

"Then it may be a good idea if we start looking around those places. It would be the perfect place to hide. No one coming around. No prying eyes."

It didn't feel quite right, but she didn't argue. As long as they got out of this place, and she could start ignoring her feelings again, everything would be okay. As it was, she was growing far too close to him for her own comfort.

Chapter Nine

The whole thing felt like a wild-goose chase. Other than knowing his ex-wife was somewhere in town—or rather, *had been*—they had little to go on. Maybe Alli had left again. Maybe she'd just wanted to throw everyone off her scent by taking the car north, then she'd come back and taken off south. It was a good maneuver—the double back. He'd used it in hundreds of his military exercises. His favorite was doubling back and moving in behind the enemy, gaining the high ground. If it was successful, there was almost a guarantee they could overcome their enemy.

Was that what Alli was doing now? Going for the high ground?

She had surprised him by coming back. He couldn't let her surprise him again. They had to be prepared for anything. She wasn't stupid. She'd never been stupid. He couldn't underestimate her, not if it meant anyone—especially Winnie—could be put in danger.

The more Waylon thought about Winnie, the worse he felt for the girl. She was just another of Alli's victims—another heart that had been left shattered in the woman's wake.

He knew all too well how it felt to be left by a parent. He and Colter had been down that road, though Wyatt and Rainier had gone through their own versions of hell when it came to their own biological parents. Some wounds never went away, they simply fell further into the past. And just when a person thought they were gone, those old wounds had a way of rising to the present and even scarring the future.

He glanced over at Christina as they made their way up the steps to the Sacajawea guest cabin. The place hadn't changed much since he had last been there. There was a model of a papoose above the door of the cabin, and there was a picture of Sacajawea and her baby on the door. He'd always liked this place; it had an air of the Old West, complete with pictures of bison and framed projectile points on the walls.

"It doesn't look like she's been here, either," Christina said, pressing her face to the glass and looking inside. "Nothing is out of place, at least as far as I can tell. It looks just like the others."

They had been all over the ranch, but there hadn't been any evidence that anyone, let alone Alli, had been to the cabins in the last week.

They were just running in circles, and he hated the feeling of impotence that filled him.

He sighed, and Christina turned to him. "It's going to be okay," she said. "At least we're checking everything we can off the list. And right now, we know that Winnie is taken care of. Gwen and Wyatt won't let her out of their sight."

He looked at her as she pushed a wayward hair out of her face. As she moved, she licked her lips, and the simple action made his body stir to life. Her lips were damp, and as he looked at them, he wondered exactly what it would be like to kiss them. She was so sexy. She was probably the kind of woman who took a kiss slow at first, taking in the moment their lips met like it was an expensive scotch—and everything could be found in the first burning sip. In that moment, a person could taste all the things that had come together to make the kiss what it was and what made it special. It was like that first kiss held the promises of what their relationship could be—both good and bad.

He couldn't deny that even just the thought of kissing her was better than any scotch in the world—and probably far more addictive.

His phone rang. It was his mother. "What's up?"

"You need to come home. Where are you?" There was a high and frantic edge to her voice that made all of his senses spark to life.

"We're not far. What's going on?"

"Is Winnie with you?" his mother asked, not answering his question.

"Oh," he said, his stomach sinking as he re-membered Wyatt's request to tell his mother that they had taken her back to their place. "She's with Wyatt."

His mother let out a long sigh. "Thank God she's all right."

"Is everything okay?"

Christina passed him a questioning glance and moved closer so she could hear his exchange with his mother.

"I was just worried when I came home and saw the door open and found Winnie's room destroyed. Did you get whatever you guys were looking for in there?"

He looked over at Christina. "No one was in her room. Were they?"

"Gwen went in there to pack her a bag and grab a few things, but she wouldn't have made a mess, and I was the last one out of the house. I *know* I locked the doors when we left. I made sure of it."

The knot in his stomach returned. "We'll be right there. Is Dad with you?"

"Yeah, he's here."

"Good." He took Christina by the hand, led her back to the truck and started the engine.

"Don't go outside the house. We found out that Alli may be in Mystery and…well, who knows what she's capable of. You both need to stay safe."

THE TRUCK BUMPED down the dirt road that led out of the back forty as Waylon tried to steer around the abundant ruts in the road. It was no wonder they'd closed these cabins down— once the snow started to fall, these roads would be nearly impassable. One bad decision, one ill-prepared couple trying to drive down it in more than a few inches of snow, and without a doubt the ranch would have another mess on their hands. People constantly underestimated Montana's wild power. She was a fickle beast. One minute it could be sunny and hot, and the next it could be snowing, with hypothermia a legitimate threat.

Alli had always hated living here, a place

with such extremes, but maybe it was because she was already living with more than enough extremes within herself. She couldn't compete with another thing like her.

When they got back to the main house, every light was on, even the strands of Christmas lights that ran down the fences and around the barn's windows. If the circumstances had been different, he would have said the place looked beautiful with its array of greens and reds, but as things stood, the cast of the red lights on the bone-white fence posts only reminded him of spilled blood.

Eloise stood at the bay window, watching out for them. She was hugging herself, and as she spotted them, she turned and called out behind her. His father came to the window and gave them a small, relieved wave.

He hadn't seen his parents scared before, especially not his father. The man was the picture of steely resolve. He was the kind of man who'd spent many a night pulling calves, only to watch them pass in his arms. Even before his years on the ranch, he'd seen so much tragedy and death thanks to his years in Vietnam. He didn't talk about his time spent in the jungles. The one time Merle had even mentioned it had been after a night of heavy drinking, when he'd told a story of men in his unit stealing the gold teeth of the dead. It had made Waylon's skin crawl. Yet it was also the moment that he'd realized he needed to serve his country.

His father had been through hell and back. He was a hero. Even as a young man, Waylon had known that was what he wanted to be as well. He wanted to right the wrongs of the generations before him. He wanted to make the world a better place. And, thanks to his dark past and the demons that filled his soul, he found an insatiable need to protect those who didn't have the power or the strength to protect themselves.

He had wanted nothing more than to follow in his father's footsteps. And though he'd found himself deep behind enemy lines in Iraq, and coming under fire to protect those he'd been ordered to serve, he'd never really felt like a hero. It was strange, but most of the time he felt like nothing more than an impostor.

It was all thanks to Alli.

He had promised to stay by her side, to keep her safe in a world that promised a million forms of danger and pain, yet when push came to shove, he had left her in the middle of Montana.

He gave a cynical chuckle at the thought. He was no hero. Heroes didn't run away.

His father pulled his mother into his arms and smoothed her gray hair. It was perhaps the most touching thing he'd ever seen his father do, to put aside his strong exterior and put the needs of the one he loved the most before his own.

Perhaps true love wasn't found in strength, but rather in moments of weakness. Moments in which the soul lay bare, when fears and insecurities were open for the world to witness and judge. Those who truly loved each other didn't disappear behind their masks of strength. No. Instead, they moved into each other's arms and found all the support they needed there.

As they got out of the truck, his mother and father rushed outside to them. "What took you so long?" Eloise pressed.

Waylon glanced down at his watch. It had taken them only ten minutes of speeding down logging roads to get back, yet she was acting as though it was a lifetime.

"Did something else happen?" he asked.

His mother shook her head.

"Eloise," his father said, taking his mom by the hand, "don't be upset with him."

"How can I not be upset with him? He and

his brother didn't bother to tell me that they had taken Winnie. You know how I feel about our children going missing."

He had nearly forgotten about the time Rainier's biological mother had kidnapped his brother. Rainier had maybe been eight or nine. His mother had shown up in the night, pulled him from his bed, and no one had realized he was missing until the morning. They had all thought the precocious boy had simply found his way out into the expanses of the ranch, but after turning over every rock, they hadn't found him.

Eloise had been beyond distraught. He'd never been able to forget watching her fall to her knees on the floor of the living room and dissolve into sobs when she had realized what had happened.

It had taken nearly two weeks, and dozens of law enforcement officers searching, but they had eventually found his brother and brought him back to the ranch. Ever since, his mother had been adamant about knowing the comings and goings of all their four children and any foster kids that were in their care. He was sure her need for that type of control was out of her misplaced guilt from letting his brother fall into the wrong hands. If something had really happened to Winnie, he would have felt the same way—and just as culpable.

"I'm sorry. It slipped my mind," Waylon said, truly humbled by his error. He could only imagine the terror that must have filled her when she came home to the scene.

Eloise nodded, but the fear and anger on her face remained. "I swear, I almost had a heart attack. I don't ask much, but if you're going to be around here, you need to follow the rules."

He had no problem following the rules—his life was dictated by them—but all he could think of was that he wouldn't really be here

long enough to worry about them. A deep sadness filled him as he realized he had only a few
days of leave left, and then he would have to
return to his world of ACUs and PT—a world
of acronyms—and a far cry from the ranch.

He pushed the thought out of his mind. He
couldn't have *feelings*. He didn't have a life that
allowed for them.

"And make sure that you guys close the doors
when you are coming and going."

"We did. I swear," Christina said. "I even
locked them."

"Wait." Waylon stared. "Were the doors open
when you came home?"

She shook her head.

"Did anyone come in the house? Any staff or
guests that you know of?"

"We don't have any guests staying. Not
since…" Eloise didn't bother finishing her sentence. "And there were only a couple of the

hands around. However, when we got home, they had only just returned after taking a couple of the horses for a trail ride. When they got back, they said they saw an open door."

"And they didn't think to close it?" Christina asked.

Eloise shook her head. "You know the trainers. Some of them may have actually been born in a barn."

Christina and Merle laughed, but all Waylon could think about was the fact that someone, maybe even Alli, had been inside the house after they had left.

"Did you call the police and report a break-in?" he asked.

"No, I wanted to check in with you guys first."

"Why don't you go ahead and call Wyatt and he can get in touch with his crew. In the meantime, I'll take a look inside. Did you touch any-thing?"

His father shook his head. "We just went in-side, realized someone had definitely been in there and then waited for you to get here. I al-ready called Wyatt. He's on his way."

"Good," Waylon said. "I'll be right back. If Wyatt gets here, let him know I'm inside." He took a few steps toward the house.

"You aren't going in alone," Christina said, hurrying to catch up.

He smiled. He wasn't sure if she was coming with him because she didn't think he could do the job or if it was because she wanted to be with him, but regardless, he was happy to have her company.

Aside from the open front door, everything in the living room was in its place, and it looked as though nothing had been disturbed—at least that he could tell. As they made their way down the hallway and toward the bedrooms, it was a different story. Winnie's bedroom light was on, casting a finger of light into the hallway, where the toys spilled out of the room. A blue teddy bear that had been on Winnie's bed the night before looked unnervingly out of place in the hall, its beady black eyes peering down the hallway toward them like some terrified witness to an unspeakable crime.

"Wyatt still has Winnie, doesn't he?" Christina asked, almost as though she were as unsettled by the reality in front of them as he was.

"Yes, they have her. She's safe," he said, but as he spoke, a new sense of urgency to find Alli and put her behind bars welled within him. They couldn't live like this—no one should live their life in fear for their or their loved ones' safety. If he didn't hurry, they would have to continue on in this terrifying reality.

Winnie's room was destroyed. Toys were scattered everywhere, pictures had been pulled off the walls and even her bedding had been pulled back and thrown to the floor. The sight of her discarded bedding made the hair rise on his arms. Maybe it was the fact that the bed was a place of safety for children—where even he had pulled the sheets over his head when he'd been afraid of monsters—but the sight was chilling.

"Thank God we had gotten her out of here," Christina said, her voice flecked with terror.

"Why would Alli turn over her daughter's room? What do you think she could have been looking for?"

Christina chewed on her bottom lip, and her gaze moved to the closet. She hurried to the small door and, pulling it open, lifted a black fireproof safe off the top shelf. Someone had left it unlocked. She set the safe on the floor and opened the lid. Inside was a collection of papers, most of which looked like deeds and a car title. She riffled through the papers, taking them out and gently stacking them on the floor.

"What are you looking for?" Waylon asked, squatting down beside her.

"Alli and I...there was only one thing our grandmother left us. We are the only ones who knew about it," she said, only half explaining her maniacal digging and stacking.

"What is it?"

She stopped for a brief second and looked up at him. "My grandmother left me a three-carat diamond ring. It's flawless. Cushion cut. Inlaid sapphires around it. It's beautiful."

"You had a three-carat diamond ring in a lockbox in a two-year-old's bedroom?"

She frowned and gave him an are-you-kidding-me kind of a look. "Don't judge me. It was in a safe at the main house—I thought this would be the safest place."

He hadn't meant to make her defensive or to

comment on anything that had to do with their child-care choices.

"That's not it," he said, trying to deescalate the situation as much as he could. "I'm just surprised you didn't keep it in your bedroom, is all."

The look on her face disappeared, and she seemed to relax slightly. "In truth, I haven't thought about the ring in a long time. My grandmother wanted me to have it as my engagement ring someday. It's beautiful, but I never thought I'd use it, so I just tucked it away in the lockbox in hopes that one day Winnie would get it."

"You thought you'd never use the ring?" The thought that Christina didn't think she would get married surprised him. She was beautiful and smart—any man would be lucky to have her in his life.

She went back to pulling out the last of the papers. In the corner was a small black velvet box, and Christina sighed with relief. "Whew. It's still here," she said, gingerly lifting the box out, as though a simple jarring could destroy the precious ring inside. "Maybe someday Winnie will have better luck than I have and she'll actually get to use this thing."

"You have to have been in a serious relationship before." He paused. "Wait, weren't you with some guy? Steve or something? Weren't you seeing him when Alli and I were dating? I thought she mentioned something about you guys."

Christina scowled at the sound of the man's name. "Steve? I haven't thought about him in years." She spun the velvet box in her fingers. "He and I, we didn't fit. You know?"

He knew all too well about not really *fitting* with a person he loved. "Did you love him?" The moment the question left his lips, he felt strange for asking. It really wasn't any of his business, but he couldn't resist the urge to know more about her.

She looked up, staring at him in silence for a moment as though she were trying to understand exactly why he'd asked her and how she would respond. "I... It's not that easy," she started, then looked back down at the box.

"It's okay to have loved someone and lost them."

"That's not it." She shook her head. "I don't know how much my sister told you about our parents, but let's just say they weren't the best examples when it came to what a healthy relationship should be. They were constantly fighting. Then they'd cheat." She spun the box again like it was a talisman that could keep the dark thoughts at bay. "I just never wanted to have a relationship like theirs."

"So you push people away?"

She sent him the sexiest guilty smile he'd

seen in all of his life. "So Alli told you a few things about me, did she?"

He laughed, the sound echoing off the empty bedroom walls. "Actually, she didn't. I picked up that little gem on my own."

She laughed, and the sound was so unexpected and beautiful that he held his breath, as though if he moved, her laughter would vanish just as quickly as it had appeared, like some skittish animal.

"I don't know how you got there, but there are some things I guess I can't deny. It's just," she said, smiling at him, "well, I don't want to waste my time falling in love with the wrong man."

Was she talking about him? Was she falling in love with him, or was she implying that she wouldn't fall in love with him because she didn't want to waste her time?

The thought made his head hurt. Women made everything so complicated. If she liked him—or didn't, for that matter—she could have just said it. She didn't have to dance around the attraction that seemed to simmer between them.

On the other hand, he wasn't about to fall on that sword by saying something. Clearly she wasn't interested in him. He stood up and started toward the door, unsure of exactly what to do other than to go.

"Wait." He turned around as a thought crossed his mind. He motioned to the ring box. "Look inside."

The box clicked as she pulled it open. She let out a long, raspy breath as though someone had punched her in the gut. "No. She didn't."

Christina turned the box so he could see. There was nothing inside. Once again, they were left with only questions.

Chapter Ten

Why would Alli ever steal the only possession that meant anything to her? Christina kept her tears in check, but they threatened to spill over her resolve at any second. It was all too much.

Christina clicked the box closed and dumped it back in the safe. The lockbox slid off her lap and onto the floor. It would have been more prudent to be more careful, as she sat in the middle of a crime scene. Yet, at the same time, she was so beyond caring. She had been through so much emotional upheaval lately, it was almost as if this all had beaten her to the point of numbness.

She looked at the black rectangular box. They wouldn't have been able to pull prints from the box, but maybe the police could pull some off the other items in the room. Then again, she doubted they would even try. The only people who knew about that ring were her and her sister. It wasn't much of a mystery who had taken it—the only question that remained was why her sister would have been so ruthless.

"Did Wyatt check out your sister's bank accounts?" Waylon asked, pulling her back to the wreckage that surrounded her.

She nodded. "He's been monitoring it, but nothing has been drawn since the day she disappeared."

"Did she empty them out before she left, or take out any large sums of money?"

"What large sums? Alli was living hand to

mouth—basically everything she made went to Winnie."

"I had been paying her alimony. Didn't she save any of that money?" he asked, his face was pinched as though he was thinking about all the money he'd given to her since their divorce.

Christina shrugged. "I don't know what my sister did with her money. I didn't have anything to do with that part of her life. But having Winnie was hard on her, both emotionally and financially."

Waylon's mouth opened and closed as if he had an idea but wasn't sure he wanted to tell her exactly what he was thinking.

"What?" she asked.

"Huh?"

"Just tell me why you are standing there guppying. There's nothing you can possibly say that I probably haven't already thought about my sister—especially after everything that's happened lately."

"Do you think that any of this has something to do with her mental health? Or do you think maybe she wanted the ring for herself? Maybe she was jealous?"

"Are you implying that you think my sister is crazy?" She tried to sound mad, but the numbness she felt made her voice flat.

"Not that harsh, but you know. She was having affairs when we were together. Maybe she was depressed about this thing with William dissolving. It could have sent her off the deep end and made her think everything and everybody is fair game."

"Are you implying that you think my sister would hurt me out of a jealous rage or something? That's silly. She wouldn't do something like that. Maybe she just wanted the ring to

sell. She may have just needed the money—
like you said."

She wasn't sure what to say, so she simply sat
watching him as he shifted his weight from one
foot to the other with discomfort. Regardless
of whatever he thought or felt about her sister,
Alli would never hurt her—at least she hoped
she wouldn't.

"You know, I gave her about forty thousand
dollars when we divided our assets during our
divorce. She should have at least been able to
put a down payment on a little place. I bet my
mother would have helped her get a place, too,
if she'd wanted. So why didn't she? I mean,
where did the money go? She's been erratic and
dangerous. What if she had other problems?"

Christina stood up and brushed off a wayward Lego that had embedded in her thigh
when she had sat down. "Do you mean you
think my sister might have been a drug ad-

dict?" she asked ever so slowly. If Waylon was as smart as she assumed he was, he would hear the warning in her tone.

"No!" he said, panic filling his voice. "No. God, why do you always have to jump to the worst conclusion first? I just was wondering if she had gotten herself into some kind of trouble. I guess, yeah, she could have been into drugs." He glanced over at her. "Is that what you think was happening? That she had some kind of drug addiction—and that's what moved her toward murder and theft?"

Christina believed this had all happened because Alli had fallen in love with William Poe. Sure, falling in love was sometimes just like being an addict—her sister had always been chasing the next hit. And toward the end, before she'd left, she hadn't let anyone or anything stand in the way of getting the man she had wanted—even when it meant killing Bianca and Monica. Yet drugs and love weren't the same—not at all. You could only do so many drugs before you overdosed.

Christina looked up into Waylon's brown eyes. He was still staring at her like he wanted some kind of sign that she agreed with his thinking. In truth, she agreed with him—Alli had more going on than anyone knew. Heck, every time they looked into her sister's activities before her disappearance they learned some new deeper, darker secret. And everything came back to men—either Waylon, William or any number of her other lovers.

Men and love were more trouble than they were worth.

Waylon took her by the hand. The sensation of his warm fingers against hers made her wonder if she was wrong. Was Waylon right, and her sister was involved in something far more sinister and dangerous than Christina had assumed? Everyone had simply presumed that Alli had done what she had out of jealousy, but what if there was something more at play? Something that could affect them all?

"You know how Alli is…or at least *was* when you were with her. She is impulsive. I guess it wouldn't surprise me if she got into something and got in way over her head," she admitted.

"There was this one time, when we were together…" He stopped, almost as though he hadn't realized that he was reminiscing until it was already out of his mouth. He looked at her as though talking about his relationship with Alli suddenly made him uncomfortable.

He gave her a sexy half grin, and it had an air of apology to it.

"You don't have to stop. We both loved her once," she said, secretly wondering if his feelings toward her had something to do with his reluctance to talk about her sister.

She hated to even think about what he felt toward her, fearing if she did it would somehow make things between them more real— and even more tense. She didn't want more of her body or her mind telling her that she needed to kiss him.

In fact, if he talked about her sister more, Christina was sure she could pull herself back to reality and out of the fantasy that seemed to fill her thoughts every time she let her mind drift. No matter how good the dream was of taking his lips, letting him lace them over her skin and down her neck, it wasn't healthy to give her daydreams any room to grow.

She drew in a long breath, and at its edges was his scent. He smelled of men's cologne and the sweet crisp scent of winter air.

"I guess right now it doesn't matter what pushed Alli to her breaking point," he said. "What does matter is the ring and Winnie's safety. After she sells that ring, it may be only a matter of hours before she comes to get her daughter. Maybe she just needed the money in order to run."

"There are all kinds of things that she could take from this ranch and sell if she wanted to make money. This can't be about that," she said, trying to find some other reasonable answer behind her sister's illogical behavior. "She had to have done this just to send me a message."

"You're right." He nodded. "Maybe she could have stolen some other things from the ranch and that's how she's been getting by. But what if someone connected some of the things that she was selling to this ranch? Maybe she had to steal something that wasn't so obvious—maybe she was afraid that someone would come to the family with information…information they wouldn't have wanted to give to the police."

"Not everyone wants to protect this family, Waylon," she said, but the words came out much harsher than she had intended. "I mean, there's more than a few people out there, just like William Poe, who would go out of their way to make sure Dunrovin fails."

He stopped her with the wave of his hand. "I know we aren't the Kennedys, Christina, but we have a lot of love and support in this community. My mother and father give a lot to charity, they bankroll the high school extra-curriculars when they can and, heck, you know how much they foster."

Waylon wasn't wrong. His family as a whole was nothing if not altruistic and kind. They were the picture of giving. Yet not everyone in the world appreciated that kind of people—and more often than not, they were the first ones to get taken advantage of. Heaven knew she had stopped more than one employee from taking advantage of Eloise. Just two months ago, they'd had a young woman apply for a job. She'd plied Mrs. Fitzgerald with a sob story about getting kicked out of her parents' home after they had caught her with a man they hadn't approved of.

Of course, Eloise had hired the girl, letting her work as a housekeeper. In only two weeks, the girl had robbed at least three guests that they knew of, to the tune of nearly two thousand dollars' worth of jewelry and cash. Eloise had covered the loss, but it had been up to Christina to fire the girl. If she hadn't, Eloise without a doubt would have kept her on.

Almost exactly the same thing had happened with Alli when she had arrived at the ranch, except instead of jewelry, she had stolen Waylon's heart.

Christina glanced over at him. He was staring at her, and there was a whisper of empathy on his face as their eyes locked.

"It's not a secret that Alli has stolen before."

"I know." She walked out of the bedroom. There was nothing more they could do here. Alli had sent her message—she wasn't coming back, and she didn't care about Christina.

"Wait," Waylon said, calling after her as she made her way down the hall. "Where are you going?"

She had no idea. She just couldn't be in the center of her sister's mess anymore. "Your brother and his team can handle this. I'm out. I'm so tired. I can't handle this...any of this."

She made her way through the living room toward her bedroom on the other side of the ranch-style house. Partway down the hall, she stopped. She didn't want to be in this house or anywhere near it for a while. Yet there was nowhere else to go. She didn't have anything but this place, and thanks to Wyatt and Gwen, she didn't even have her niece to keep her company.

All she had was Waylon and the feelings that flooded her whenever he was near.

She turned back to him and, taking him by the hand, pulled him toward the front door. "Let's get out of here."

"What?" he asked, but he didn't resist her leading him out of the house and to the truck. "Wyatt's on his way."

"Whatever," she said, motioning for him to get in as she made her way around to the driver's side. "He can handle this."

Mr. and Mrs. Fitzgerald were standing in the yard next to Wyatt, who was sitting in his squad car. He gave them a two-finger wave as they made their way out of the house.

She sighed, letting go of Waylon's hand as they changed direction toward his brother's car. They were never going to be able to get out of this place now. Why was it, when all she wanted to do was run away, there was always something that had to be done, or someone who needed something from her?

No wonder Waylon had taken the chance to escape when he could. And it was no wonder, now that he was back, all he wanted to do was leave. This place was like a giant pit of quicksand from a cheesy action movie. Put even a toe in, or give a little bit of your heart to the ranch, and pretty soon you were in over your head, and the more you struggled to pull your way out, the deeper you sank.

Waylon walked ahead of her as she trudged toward Wyatt. She could hear him telling his brother about the state of the bedroom and the missing ring.

Wyatt looked around his brother and waved her over. "Do you have a picture of the ring we could give to the pawnshops in the area?"

So even he thought her sister was going to sell it. Perhaps it was time she saw her sister for the person she really was—everyone else seemed to get it. They all saw Alli for the terrible person she had become, and they weren't tethered to the past by their emotions. She had made choices that were unforgivable. She had cost people their lives and others their families. She had cost Winnie her mother, and she had cost Christina a sister.

Some things were unforgivable—and heartbreaking. It was time that she truly let go of the person she had always thought her sister was. Alli simply wasn't the girl Christina had known; rather, she had become some warped and heartless stranger.

Waylon put his hand on the small of her back. "Do you have a picture of the ring?" he asked, repeating Wyatt's question.

She shook her head. "I don't have one," she said, trying to ignore the pain in her chest. "But the ring is one of a kind. It's a three-carat cushion-cut diamond inlaid with blue sap-phires." Her voice cracked as she talked. It was unlikely she would ever see the ring again, and it was the last tangible thing that connected to her grandmother.

"Don't worry," Eloise said, coming over and wrapping her in her arms. "The boys will find it and your sister. She couldn't have gone far. It'll turn up, and we'll get this all figured out. We'll find it."

The way Eloise repeated herself made it ob-vious that even she didn't believe what she was saying, but Christina appreciated the attempt at comforting her.

"And who knows," Eloise said, giving Waylon a questioning look. "Maybe you will be getting a new ring soon."

What in the hell was the woman talking about?

Christina pulled herself out of the woman's

grasp. There was no possible way Eloise could have known what Waylon felt for her, or what she felt for him. Heck, she barely knew what *she* felt toward the man. Sure, he was good-looking, and she kept imagining him between the sheets, but that was where things ended. She didn't have the time or emotional space to deal with a man like him.

She turned and started to walk away, unable to stand Eloise's teasing look or the surprise on Waylon's face. She couldn't do this anymore. She couldn't stand all the emotions that seemed to fill this place. Everyone had an agenda, and none of them were making her any less confused.

"Where are you going?" Eloise called after her.

She didn't turn around. Instead, she waved behind her.

"Wait," Waylon called. She heard the crunch

of gravel as he jogged to catch up. "With your sister out there, I don't think it's a good idea for you to be going anywhere alone. What are you thinking, anyways?"

She got in the truck and waited for him as he jumped in next to her, but she didn't say anything.

"Are you going to tell me where you're going?" Waylon asked again, pressing her for answers that she wasn't ready to give.

Christina started the truck, letting it rumble for a moment as it warmed up, and tried to collect her thoughts. The clouds that collected on the mountains had started to thicken and take on the dangerous gray color of a looming storm. It was an eerie reminder of her life. Just when she thought she had figured herself out and was on a forward path, storm clouds threatened to overtake her and make her lose sight of who she thought she was and what she thought she wanted. Yet with storms came the refreshing promise of rain, as long as one could survive the winds and lightning.

She sighed at the thought.

"What?" Waylon asked, looking over at her.

"Nothing."

She looked up to the clouds one more time. She couldn't decide who, exactly, was the most destructive force in her life, between her sister—who left pain and chaos in her wake—and Waylon, who, equally sexy and frustrating, seemed to make promises with his touch and his gaze that she knew he couldn't keep. At least with her sister there was a hope that when they found her and she went to prison, maybe she could go back to the girl Christina had once known. If Christina allowed Waylon any deeper into her heart, she would be left with nothing but an identity in tatters.

If she fell for him, her whole life would have

to change again. And she couldn't change what she wanted or who she was for him.

The gravel of the driveway slipped and spattered as she gunned the engine and they roared out of the ranch and into the vast expanses of the pastures. Regardless of the threatening storms that rested on the horizon, she needed to get out of the place and escape her reality, if only for a few moments. She needed to find a sense of peace.

Waylon reached over and put his hand on her thigh. The action was so unexpected and his hand was so warm that she jerked the wheel slightly, and the truck drifted off the road, catching a bit of the grass, which made a whipping sound against the metal.

"Whoa, cowgirl. You okay? Are you sure you're up for driving?" he asked, but he didn't move his hand from her thigh.

She shook her head and tried to ignore the

way her heart thrashed in her chest as the heat of his touch intensified on her leg and radiated up to more forbidden places. She wasn't going to find peace with him touching her like that.

"I'm sorry about Winnie's room. I'm sure that Wyatt will pull something usable from it," Waylon said, having completely misread her emotions. "And at the very least, we got Winnie out in time."

Though he was thinking about something far different than her, she was glad he was talking about something that didn't involve his hand on her thigh, or the way she didn't really want him to move it, no matter how much he should. It felt so good to be touched by a man—and not any man, but Waylon Fitzgerald. The man she'd sworn to hate for a lifetime—but after having met him, she couldn't even manage the feat for a day.

Did he have that effect on all women?

He was so serious, but under the facade was something so lovable, so kind and unexpectedly gentle that it was hard not to fall. Not that she was falling. No. She was just dipping her toes in the cool waters of Waylon Fitzgerald.

After a few miles, they hit the deserted wilds of an old logging road. She'd been on it before, but only a few times, and when the road forked, she passed him a questioning glance. Without a word, he smiled and gestured to the left with his chin.

Apparently, he was more than willing to take a minute and get lost together.

She followed the dirt road deeper into the timber, until they were high on the mountain and the clouds seemed so close that if they reached out the window they could have touched them. She'd always loved this part of living in Montana, where it seemed like in just a few minutes all were within a finger space of heaven.

Bits of wet snow started to flutter down from the clouds, a tentative warning of what could come. Yet instead of turning around and getting off the hill that promised nothing but icy roads and danger if the storm cut loose, Christina pushed the truck deeper into the depths of nowhere.

She glanced over at Waylon to see if she was making him nervous.

For once, she could understand his desire to constantly be on the move. It was so much easier to live in the moment, to let the wind be her guide.

The wet snow collected on the windshield, finally forcing her to turn on the wipers. Before the first pass moved over the glass, one front tire hit a rut, sending them jumping in the bench seat. Waylon had been jostled closer, making her heart race.

She veered into a pullout next to the narrow

road and threw the truck into Park. "Let's go," she said.

"What? Wait," Waylon said, grabbing her hand and stopping her from getting out of the truck. "Where are you going?"

Christina motioned feebly toward the small game trail beside them. "Let's hike."

He frowned. "We can't hike. It's starting to snow, and it's going to be dark soon. What's going on with you?" He took hold of their entwined fingers with his free hand. "What's the matter? Is there something you're not telling me about you and Alli? You know you can tell me anything. I'm not going to judge you."

She didn't know if she believed him, and she most certainly didn't dare admit the thing bothering her the most was her growing feelings for him.

Waylon reached up and pushed a stray hair behind her ear as she turned to him. She looked up into his face. The gray clouds were reflected in his dark brown irises, but in his eyes the storm didn't have the same ominous tone; instead, his eyes only seemed to promise that with one simple blink the storm would be gone and the sun would shine once again.

She leaned into his hand, letting him cup her face.

He moved closer, his breath hot against her lips, and he waited, almost as if he wasn't sure if she would move out of his touch. But she didn't move. All she wanted was him. His touch. His lips against hers. His hands on her skin.

She wanted all of him.

His lips grazed hers, making her need for him roar to life. She wrapped her arms around his neck and let his kiss overtake her. She had imagined this moment, but it was nothing like the reality. His tongue moved against hers, pressing and teasing and making her think of other things that she wanted him to do with his tongue.

Leaning back, she pressed her back against the truck's door. Reaching under her, he lifted her hips and pulled her down so she could lie flat on the truck's bench seat. He smiled as he looked down at her.

"Have I ever told you how beautiful I think you are?"

She giggled, covering her face with her hands. It had been so long since a man had talked to her like that, or since a man had given her *that* look. She felt silly as she gazed up at him from between her fingers. She should have been so much more confident and secure—she was old enough to know how to act around a man who wanted her.

His smile grew impossibly wider as she smiled up at him. Instead of reaching up to lower her hands, he leaned down and pulled her gingham shirt out from her jeans, exposing her stomach. He ran his rough, calloused hand over the soft skin of her belly, making her skin tingle to life as she grew wet with desire.

She groaned, the sound thick and guttural, at the sensations that threatened to overtake her. She couldn't remember the last time she had wanted a man as badly as she wanted Waylon, here and now.

"Waylon," she whispered, the sound as rough but tender as his hands.

He didn't answer. Instead, he leaned down and kissed around her navel. Her hips arched upward, her body responding on instinct. Yes. She wanted this. She needed this. It had been too long. She needed to feel alive again.

He sat up and slipped his fingers from under her shirt, unbuttoning each button as he slowly moved up her stomach and toward her breasts. Opening the last button, he let her shirt fall open on the seat next to her, exposing her black lace bra. He sat back and just looked at her for a minute.

Vulnerability wasn't even close to what she was feeling. No. It was something rawer and more frightening. She sucked in her stomach and pushed up her breasts in an attempt to make her body look as beautiful as possible, and to hide the effect of the years of hard work and ranch life.

"Stop," he said, his voice gentle and understanding. "You don't have to be something you're not with me. You're perfect just as you are."

She could have sworn her heart stopped for a brief moment as his words melted into her. Just when she thought she couldn't possibly be more attracted to him.

He ran his fingers up her abdomen and over the top of her bra, moving between her legs and leaning down. Pushing back the edges of her bra, he pulled her nipple into his mouth. He sucked it, before moving to the other side. She arched her back, letting him feel the heat that he was making erupt from her center.

"Waylon," she whispered. His name tasted like cotton candy on her tongue.

He felt so good between her thighs, the weight of him pressing against her. Rubbing as he rolled her nipple over his lips.

"I want you," she whispered, her voice hoarse with desire. "Please, Waylon."

He leaned back, letting go of her nipple and giving her a wolfish smile. "Are you sure?"

Her body screamed yes, but there was a nagging thought in the back of her mind, in the area where logic reigned, that screamed no—this was a bad idea. For her, when two bodies came together, the hearts were quick to follow. And, in this case, her heart was entirely too close to falling over the precipice into love as it was.

This was a bad idea. Letting her body win was a rookie mistake—a mistake made by those who hadn't become cynical about love, those who still believed the world was a fairy tale and when it came to following the heart, there was always hope. In other words, love was for people who weren't like her. She was too strong for love.

She put her hand on his chest and gently pressed him off her. "Wait," she said, the weak resolve she felt sounded even weaker when voiced. "I want you. This, Waylon."

"I want you, too," he said, the wolfish look in his eyes still feeding on his lust. "You know what?"

She was glad he was changing the subject, and that for at least a moment, she had time to think with her head and not her body. "What?"

He sat back as he ran his hands over her stomach. "You are so freaking sexy."

She giggled like a teenager even though her mind protested the adolescent sound. She had to fight the urge to go backward in time and continue to follow her lusty impulses.

"And?" she teased.

"And I'm glad that you are who you are. You are so strong and kind. And I love that you always tell me the truth. Whether or not I want to hear it. I appreciate it—your honesty."

His words struck a raw nerve, pulling Winnie and his family's omission to the forefront of her mind.

If he was attracted to her for her honesty and forthrightness, then he didn't know who she really was—in fact, she was exactly the opposite of the woman he assumed she was, the woman he wanted her to be.

Forget falling into each other's arms; if they were even going to be friends, he needed to know the truth—no matter the consequences.

Chapter Eleven

Waylon didn't have a clue where things had gone wrong. One minute he was feeling her quake beneath his touch, begging him to continue with the motions of her hips. She had looked and acted as though she had been enjoying herself just as much as he had, but in the next moment she had pushed him away.

He ached as he thought about how badly he had wanted her, and how sweet she had tasted. She carried the flavor of peppermint gum and sugar on her lips, and it was a heady mix. Every kiss he searched for the same flavor, pushing

deeper and harder. Her touch was intoxicating—it was something he was never going to
forget.

It was funny, but he'd never really thought
about a kiss before; for him a kiss was a kiss
was just a kiss. At least it had been with every
woman before Christina. With her, it was entirely different. It was almost as if when their
lips came together, they were the keys to un-
locking another existence. A world where love
was free to move unchecked by time, space or
the needs of others.

Yet she mustn't have felt the same way. If she
had, they would be covered in sweat and making believe they were the only two people in
the world.

What was wrong with him?

He ran his hands over his face and sighed as
they bumped down the country road that led
back to the ranch. It had been stupid to fall into

her body. Now everything between them would be even more tense than it had been before. It was going to be a long few days until he would have to leave.

Was that why she had pushed him away? Because she was afraid he would leave her in the cold?

He wanted to reach over and touch her again, to feel her tense under his fingers, but he resisted the urge. Her body was so far from him that she pressed hard against the door, as though she couldn't get enough distance. His touch was probably the last thing she wanted right now.

He opened his mouth to tell her they could try to do the long-distance thing if she wanted, but he stopped. Nothing like that would ever work. Long-distance relationships were almost always doomed to fail. There was no way people could really get to know another just based on talking. So much of what happened between two people was in the body language. Just like when they had parked. Much of what she wanted to tell him was in her eyes, in the way she had looked up at him from behind her thick black eyelashes and the way her hips had pressed against him, showing him how she ached for him just as badly as he ached for her.

She had wanted him. Right up until the point they had started to talk. He shouldn't have opened his mouth—it always got him in trouble. Though it wasn't a bad thing they had taken a step back. If she wasn't feeling it, then she wasn't feeling it. He wasn't about to rush her, and thinking about it now that he had a clearer head, it was a relief it hadn't happened. He liked and wanted her, and they could have a thing while he was here, but there was no future in their relationship.

She didn't seem like the type who would want anything to do with his lifestyle. He was a military nomad, moving from one place to another based on his orders. It took a special woman to want to follow her spouse around, and that wasn't saying anything about what happened when he was deployed. And deployment in his life was never an if—it was always a when.

She deserved a man who could dote on her, who could give her the world and everything that she wanted from it. That couldn't be him. His life was already promised to the country, and her life was promised to the care of Winnie. Plus, she'd made it clear that the ranch was her life. Or had she?

"Do you ever think about leaving Dunrovin?" Waylon wasn't sure he wanted to know the truth, but he couldn't keep thinking in circles about Christina. He needed at least a soft yes or no when it came to the feelings growing within him.

She nibbled on her lip, making him think of

their lips touching and her taste. His body quivered to life, but he tried to control himself.

"I've thought about moving away, but now that's not really an option." She sucked in a long breath and exhaled it slowly as she gave him a searching look. "Though that may change. I guess we just never know what the future will bring, do we?" Her expression was strange, and it reminded him of a person who was trying in vain to keep a secret.

He'd seen that kind of look before, normally when he was interrogating people. Just a few months before, he had been the lead investigator on an attempted murder at Bragg. According to the wife, her husband had come home late after a night of heavy drinking with his buddies. It wasn't an uncommon occurrence, and a fight had erupted about his behavior. Allegedly, the man had taken a small hatchet and come after the woman, threatening to kill her.

She had been lucky, walking away with only a few scratches and bruises.

As Waylon had interrogated the husband, the man had been evasive, never really wanting to answer his questions. He had given Waylon the same look Christina was giving him now—a look that told of deep secrets. That look had made all the difference. Going back to the crime scene, he'd reconstructed the events and eventually found the man hadn't been the one wielding the hatchet—it had been the wife.

If that was what marriage was like behind closed doors, he could do without it. He cringed as he thought about how, from the outside, most marriages were the picture of the American dream, yet when you opened the door and delved into the reality, many were the stuff of nightmares. His relationship with Alli, while not murderous, had definitely been just as dark.

"The future..." He started but paused as he

tried to collect his thoughts. "There's only a few things in life we can control. Hearts and futures aren't on the list of things we can conquer. You know what I mean?"

She turned the steering wheel, pulling into the ranch's parking lot. She threw the truck into Park and dropped her hands in her lap. For a moment, she just sat there silently staring, but she finally looked up at him. "Conquer? That's not something that applies to one's heart. You can change it, you can fill it and you can own it—at least for a time—but you can never keep what isn't yours."

What exactly did she mean? Was she trying to hint that he had part of her heart or that he didn't? Why did she have to talk in riddles all the time? Women were so complicated, especially Christina. She was a mystery to him, and as much as it should have gotten under his skin, it only made him want to get to know her that much more. It would be an incredible thing to have even a part of her heart.

He moved to touch her, but before he could, she stepped out of the truck and rushed toward the barn. As she opened the door, he could see his mother standing inside, grabbing a flake of hay and stepping toward one of the older mares' stalls. Eloise stopped and turned as Christina said something, and dropped the hay she was holding. Turning slowly, Eloise looked over her shoulder at Waylon. She looked surprised, but then as she noticed him watching, she gave him a weak, empathetic smile. She mouthed what looked like *okay* as she turned back to Christina.

Something was very, very wrong, and based on his mother's expression, whatever was going on wasn't something he was going to like.

He made his way toward the two women in the barn. He couldn't handle the looks or the strange tension that seemed to reverberate through the air.

"What's going on?" he asked, his gaze moving from one woman to the other, but neither seemed able to meet it.

"Are you absolutely sure this is the best time?" his mother asked, looking toward Christina.

"There's never going to be a right time, but if we wait any longer..." Christina finally looked to him, and there were tears welling in her eyes. "I'm so sorry, Waylon."

"Sorry for what?" He hated the way she was looking at him, with pity and hurt in her eyes. The last time anyone had given him that look had been the day he'd been taken from his biological family. The woman with child protective services had given him that exact same look... it was the look that told him nothing was ever going to be the same again.

Part of him wanted to turn around and run. It

could have been his instinct taking over, or perhaps it was the pain of his past, but he couldn't just stand there and take a blow he could see coming.

He started to turn, but his mother grabbed him by the arm, stopping him. "I know you, Waylon. This isn't something you want to run away from. At least not yet." She let go of him and gave him a weak smile, which helped to quell some of the panic that was welling within him. "Just listen."

He balled his fists but then slowly relaxed his fingers. "Fine. What in the hell is going on?"

Christina took his hands in hers. His mother gave him an approving nod.

"Everything's going to be okay, Waylon. Nothing has to change," Christina started.

The knot of nerves in his belly tightened. Now he was sure everything was about to flip on its head.

"My sister made a lot of mistakes. You know most of them. Heck, you were the victim of most of her poor decisions," Christina said, running her fingers over the back of his hand. "But there was one mistake…well, not mistake, but rather an error in judgment that…well… We all… We…"

"We are just as much at fault as Alli," his mother said, her voice high with nerves. "We should have told you sooner. Years ago, but—"

"Wait," he said, raising his hand. "*What*, exactly, should you have told me years ago?"

"It's about Winnie…" Christina mumbled.

His heart stopped at the sound of the little girl's name.

Christina looked up at him, and her eyes were filled with apologetic fear. "Winnie is yours, Waylon. She's your daughter."

Chapter Twelve

The Dog House Bar was packed, and as Waylon walked in, he had to weave his way around the throngs in order to find the only open seat at the bar. He shouldn't have taken Christina's truck without asking her, but considering the bomb she had just dropped on him, he couldn't feel bad. In fact, all he felt was the sting of betrayal.

How the hell had his family come to the decision that it was okay to keep a secret—not just a secret, but an entire child's existence—from him?

His mother and Christina had made feeble attempts to apologize as he'd walked out of the barn. They had both sworn they had wanted to tell him before and they were just doing as Alli had begged them to do, but all their excuses had fallen on deaf ears. There was no reasonable explanation that could justify the fact they had kept his being a father a secret.

He was someone's *father*.

He was Winnie's *dad*.

He waved at the bartender. "Whiskey."

The bartender poured the shot and handed it over. "Anything else?"

He motioned toward the taps. "And I'll take a Coors."

The guy looked at him with a raise of the brow. "Rough night?"

"If I told you, you wouldn't believe me."

The guy laughed, poured Waylon's beer and slid it down the bar to him, not slopping a single drop. "That one's on the house, but I'll lay a bet to say your story probably wouldn't even compare to some of the things I've had people tell me."

He snorted—that, he could believe. Booze and secrets always seemed to spill together. It was one of the reasons he rarely drank. He hated to open up the doors to his heart any wider than necessary, but in his defense, it was a rare day when someone learned they had a two-year-old daughter. A daughter who had already made a place for herself in his heart... but he doubted he could make room for her in his life.

What in the hell was he going to do now?

He downed the first shot. The whiskey burned his throat, but he welcomed the feeling. He pulled air through his nose, letting the burn move through him completely. It had been a long time since his last drink, and as the sensation overtook him, he relished it.

He was a father. The thought felt as airy and burning as the alcohol on his breath. How could it have happened?

He smirked. The last time he and Alli had been together had been before he'd filed for the divorce. He stopped. No... Wait... There *had* been one more time...one time after the divorce had been finalized. It had been the night he'd told her he was leaving for the military. It had been their farewell to one another. One last time. One last night together.

Apparently, it had been one heck of a farewell.

He wasn't sure whether or not he should laugh or jump into action, but he wasn't going to feel sorry for himself—he couldn't—and he wasn't going to let his daughter go through a childhood like his. At least not as far as being abandoned or mistreated. She'd be fine at the ranch, just as he had been. It was a great place to grow up, a place surrounded by horses, water and the shielding strength of the Rocky Mountains. Yet he couldn't be there. He had a job. He had a life. He had people to protect—people needed him. That was to say nothing of his commitment to the military—it was his everything. The army was him.

He ran his hands over his face, stopping for a moment to scratch at the stubble on his cheeks. He needed to shave, but then again, he needed a lot of things—starting with a family he could trust to always tell him the truth.

Seriously, how could they have done this to him? And why? He just couldn't make sense of it. Maybe they were trying to protect him, but even then, from what? A child wasn't something that he should be protected from. Was it that they thought he wasn't ready for a kid?

Did they think he would be like his biological parents and just abandon the kid? They
were wrong if they thought he could put a kid
through a life like his.

He sighed as he thought about his first run-in
with Winnie, when she'd fallen out of the tree.
Sure, he might not have had a clue about how
to raise a kid, but that didn't mean he wasn't
willing to learn. Or was he? He tented his fingers over his beer and stared into the foam. Two
bubbles rose, almost staring back up at him,
and he shook the glass. He didn't need anyone
or anything else to judge him—or his ability
to be a decent father.

He was more than able to be a father. He
could handle the responsibility. He could be a
dad—far worse men than him did it every day.
He could do the whole thing far better than any
one of them. He'd sign Winnie up for ballet and

T-ball. She could even get into hockey like he had when she got older.

As he thought about all the things he wanted to do with Winnie, he realized the immense time commitment it would take to raise a two-year-old. She wasn't in school or day care. Even if he started her in some kind of program, he would still have to take her there and pick her up. At Bragg, he would be completely on his own with her—there would be no extra sets of hands to shuttle her around or make sure she got to where she needed on time.

And all that was without taking his schedule into consideration. In the last three years, he had been deployed nearly a third of the time. If he reenlisted, it would probably be the same. That meant Winnie would constantly be waiting for him to come home.

If only Alli had just told him. He stopped. She probably hadn't wanted to share the kid with him—or play pass-the-kid-around. Though they had spent one last night together, they really hadn't ended things on a good note; if they had added a kid to the mix, it would have undoubtedly made things between them worse. And when parents fought, it was always the kid who paid.

He didn't agree with the lie, but for a brief second he could almost understand why they had done what they had. Winnie didn't deserve to be some pawn in a game of divorce. At least Winnie was being raised with the love and safety his family provided—Alli had given the girl that much of a leg up. It would have been all too easy for her to simply disappear with the baby and never look back. Yet she had decided to let the girl be a part of his family's life—if not his. Then again, maybe it was just her easiest option. His family had given her a free ride in exchange for the time they got with the secret child.

The thought of how much she must have hated him made his chest ache. She didn't trust him, and, well, he certainly didn't trust her. As it turned out, the mistrust he felt had been completely justified.

Now that she had disappeared, the burden of the child should have fallen on him, but she had chosen her sister—and to still keep the truth hidden. She could have simply called him, left a message and let him handle things. Yet she hadn't, and the thought made him ache even more.

It might have been her plan all along, to come back for her daughter the moment she thought the police were off her trail. If she kept Waylon out of it, kidnapping the girl would have been easier—at least she knew no one was threatening to take Winnie away from the ranch or from Christina. Alli probably was just waiting for the right moment to strike. First, she took the ring, got a little mad money, and then she and his daughter would be gone.

Alli was the epitome of selfishness. Everything she had ever done, every choice she had ever made—even in marrying him in the first place—had been to advance herself and her desires. She didn't have a selfless bone in her body—apparently not even when it came to her child.

Bottom line, she couldn't get her hands back on Winnie. It was impossible to know what she was capable of, and no matter what the future had in store for him, he couldn't let Winnie's safety be compromised—by anyone. Even if she wasn't his daughter, her safety would have been number one, yet now that he knew the truth, it made everything more real and more immediate.

His daughter…the words echoed in his mind. It felt so strange to hear them rattling around in his thoughts, to feel the weight of the words on his shoulders. Yet, strangely enough, he welcomed the weight. It was nice to think he wasn't alone in the world and just maybe he could keep the girl safe.

He moved to stand up, then stopped—he could save his daughter from many things, but her mother was not someone he could completely protect her from. The woman would always have a place in the girl's heart and she would figure out a way into her life. Even if that meant she would ransack her daughter's belongings for a ring that he assumed Alli wanted just for the money.

There had to be something else missing. Something else going on.

He normally loved this part of an investigation, where he searched for the key to the puzzle. Yet, with so much at stake, he hated this case. It was best that Wyatt was the one investigating this. There was no way he could remain objective now. Especially if Alli laid a finger on their daughter.

The word echoed again, and this time it didn't sound as foreign.

He took a long drink of his beer. There was no way he was ready to go back to the ranch and his waiting family. He wasn't ready to face their apologetic faces and downcast gazes. It would take a long time to get used to the word *daughter*, but it would take even longer to trust them again. Trust would have to be earned. Yet, if he looked into Christina's glacial-blue eyes, a color so clean and pure that it seemed bottomless, he wasn't sure he could continue being as resolute as he felt now. It was easy to be angry when he didn't have to face her, when he didn't have to hear her soft voice.

If his brothers had asked him to keep a secret, as Alli had done with Christina, he probably would have made the same choice she had. He had to respect her and his family's honor and loyalty—albeit to the wrong person.

Of course, this all could have come back to the fact that they didn't want to lose the baby, either. They really must have believed what they were doing was for the best.

There was no getting around it—he had to talk to them.

He moved to stand up but stopped as he turned to face the main bar area. Sitting two tables over from him was William Poe. There was a woman with him, with dark hair and heavy makeup; she looked like the woman he and Christina had seen at Poe's house the day before. Lisa.

He turned back to the bar and waved down

the bartender. The man dried a pint glass as he made his way over. "Need another round?"

He waved him off. "Nah. But, hey, do you know that guy over there?" He pointed at William.

"Sure, that's William Poe. I think he does something for the county. He's in here a lot. Why?" The guy leaned in closer in an effort to keep their conversation a little more private.

"You know the woman he's with?"

"Yeah," the guy said with a nod. "Her name's Lisa. Lisa Chase, I think."

"Are they in here together often?"

The guy shrugged. "She just started hanging around with him in the last month or so. Poe's always got a new chippie on his arm. I'm sure she'll be replaced in another few weeks. Usually I don't even bother learning their names."

"Why this time? I mean, why do you know her name?"

"She's the one who's been paying the tab."

It made sense that the one thing the bartender would care about was the person paying the bill. Waylon would have felt the same way in the guy's position. Especially in a place like this.

"Does William normally buy the drinks for his dates?"

The bartender nodded. "The word on the street is that his wife's assets are in probate and he's been spending a lot of money trying to track down the woman who killed her— at least that's what I heard him say. You hear about the case?"

It was a relief the guy didn't know who Waylon was or what his connection was to the local events. There was a certain amount of freedom in anonymity.

"What about it?" he asked.

"Apparently, one of Poe's exes went batty.

Killed his mistress, who was a local veterinar-
ian, and his wife. Bloody business when it came
to the wife." He made the motion of slicing a
neck. "But hey, at least it was quick. When I
go out, I'd choose that over cancer any day."

Waylon couldn't help but agree with the dude.
He'd seen more than his fair share of death.
The worst had been seeing bits of flesh stuck
to a mud wall after a suicide bomber had det-
onated in Tikrit. If nothing else, though, that
type of death was dehumanizing—if he didn't
think about it, the bits of flesh didn't add up to
a person. It was that thought alone that had allowed him to keep his sanity.

He thumbed the rim of his pint glass. He probably needed therapy. It was probably one of the
reasons his family hadn't wanted him to know
about Winnie. With a life like his, it would be
challenging to have a normal relationship with
a child. He would always be overly protective,

wanting to make sure his daughter was cared for and out of harm's way. It was the reality of any parent who had seen the worst and come back to civilian life.

He couldn't blame them for wanting to protect the child—not from the world, but from him.

He took out a fifty and laid it on the bar. "Thanks for the drinks, and the information. If you hear anything else about William and his crazy ex, my name's Waylon. You can get ahold of me at Dunrovin."

The guy's eyes widened with surprise as he must have put two and two together. "Waylon? Waylon Fitzgerald?"

He gave a tight nod and turned away before the bartender asked him any more questions. As of late, the only thing he had in high supply were questions—what he didn't need was more being flung at him.

Thankfully, as he made his way through the

bar, William and Lisa were too busy making out to notice him. The way they were completely lost in each other's faces made his stomach churn. William's wife had just died, yet here he was flaunting his newest fling in public.

He never wanted to be that kind of guy who moved from one woman to the next without a thought. No. He wanted one woman for the rest of time.

For a second he could think only of Christina, and how beautiful she had looked lying back on the truck's bench seat. And though he was annoyed at her for the secret she had kept, he couldn't help but imagine her porcelain skin and how it had felt to kiss the soft lines of her belly and the arc of her ribs. He'd screwed up his chance to be with her. In all ways it was as if he was the dark and she was the light—they were in perfect complement.

If he played his cards right, they could come to some kind of agreement when it came to the child, but finding himself in agreement with that woman was almost as unlikely as finding a unicorn. Perhaps it was the tension that always seemed to reverberate between them, but when it came to Winnie, he had a feeling the only common ground they would find would be the fact they each loved the child and wanted to keep her safe.

Chapter Thirteen

Christina stood by the window, watching and waiting for Waylon to come back. He had every right to be angry with her—and she wouldn't have been too surprised if she got a call that her truck had been abandoned in front of the airport. He probably hated them all right now, but most likely no one more than her.

She should have convinced Alli to tell him before, but her sister wasn't the kind who backpedaled once her mind was made up. Sure, Christina could have gone around her sister and told Waylon, but until now it would have done far more harm than good. Or at least she had thought it would. She wasn't so sure anymore.

The more she thought about the wrong they had done Waylon, and the more minutes that ticked by, the more she was convinced Waylon had run away. He had done it before. She couldn't blame him. Sometimes the only thing a person could do when they had been repeatedly broken was run. It was the only effective way she had ever learned to protect her heart— and he had probably learned the same lesson.

Her thoughts went to when she was in the truck with him, lying on the bench seat and looking up into his eyes. She had been right to stop things from going any further, but now she regretted her choice. Well, kind of regretted it. Sure, it made things easier now that he was apparently gone, yet she wished she had taken the chance to live a little. She couldn't help but imagine what it would have been like to have him further his advance, and to have him kiss places that even now begged for his touch.

She moved to the chair across the living room and sat down in the dark, still watching for him, though it was more out of desperation than an actual belief.

It felt good to sit alone in the dark. It was the first time in what felt like an eternity that she had a moment that wasn't filled with talk about what had happened and what they could do to fix things. There was always something that required her attention and action. She didn't mind when it was about Winnie, but she never had a moment to herself anymore.

She closed her eyes and drew in a long breath. This was what Waylon's life was probably like—quiet and serene. She could understand if he didn't want to take over the care of his daughter if this was what he was used to. It would be an extreme change to go from living alone in the routine of the military to caring for a two-year-old he barely knew.

He was probably scared out of his wits.

She had been scared, too, when she had read Alli's note designating her Winnie's appointed guardian. Even though she had been there for all of Winnie's life, the thought of just picking up where her sister had left off had been more than terrifying. Though she hadn't had the time to pay her own feelings too much attention. No, she had only one choice—take the girl and raise her, or give her up. She would never give up her niece. Never.

Yet if Winnie went with her father, it wouldn't be Christina's choice. It would be his, his decision whether or not he would whisk his daughter away. She had to accept it—there was no sense in going to court to fight over custody when in the end it would undoubtedly be given to the biological father. He was a good man, a

244 of 388 (document id

good provider and Winnie's closest relative. She couldn't compete with him—she owned nothing but one beat-up old truck and she trained horses, which paid her bills but not much else.

She ran her hands over her face, looking out at the moon between her open fingers.

Her breath hitched in her throat, and she couldn't control the sobs that overtook her as she thought about Winnie sitting beside Waylon in a plane, flying to a state where she'd never been and where Christina was unlikely to see her. Sure, they might have the occasional week and maybe a holiday here and there, but it would be nothing in comparison to the time they'd had together over the last few years. Basically, she would lose the girl forever.

She dabbed at the tears that poured down her cheeks. She couldn't bear the thought of losing her niece, but she also couldn't risk her safety, and she couldn't make choices on Winnie's behalf.

If Waylon ran away, as a woman who longed to feel his touch and be held in his arms, she would be broken. Yet, as Winnie's guardian, she couldn't help the feeling of freedom and relief at the thought that he might have gone. She shook her head at the realization that she could be so selfish. Even if he left, she couldn't keep Winnie. Not as her own child. No, not now that the truth was out. From this day on, Waylon would be Winnie's father and she would only ever be merely Winnie's aunt. Nothing more.

The girl would need her father to help her learn how to tie her shoes and to ride a bike, and maybe someday she would need him to walk her down the aisle.

The thought only made Christina's tears come down that much harder, and she gasped for air as her emotions moved through her un-

checked—so much that she didn't realize Waylon was standing next to her until he gave her
shoulder a soft squeeze.

"Christina, are you okay? Did something happen?"

She stood and buried herself inside his arms.
He smelled of liquor and the woody aroma of
a bar, but she didn't care. He was here. He had
come back to her. To them. He hadn't run away,
even though it would have been all too easy to
disappear into the night.

"I'm so sorry, Waylon. I'm so sorry," she said
between sobs. Her tears wet his neck and made
their skin slick, but she didn't move.

He sighed. The sound was heavy and slow,
the sound of someone who might have been
just as confused and upset as she was.

She leaned back, looking up into his face. He
gave her a smirk, the one he seemed to reserve
only for her, as it so rarely made an appearance

except when they were alone. She loved that smile, the way his eyes met hers and how, in that moment, he could make all her fears disappear.

He cupped her face with both hands, wiping away her tears with his thumbs. The feeling of his rough fingers against her soft cheeks made the need she felt for him intensify. She wanted him. All of him. All the time. Yet she would have to be satisfied with only this moment. He would have to leave in a few days, taking her world and her heart with him.

But they had tonight.

She could take this one chance to make him hers and to become his.

"I'm sorry I didn't tell you. I couldn't—"

"I get it. Let's leave it at that," he interrupted. He kept running his thumbs over her cheeks. "You did what you had to do."

The way he said the words made her wonder

if there was some hidden meaning, like he was going to do what *he* thought he had to do. But she had no idea what exactly that would entail.

She opened her mouth to ask him what his plans were, but she changed her mind and clamped her mouth shut. She didn't want to know. It would only ruin this moment. There would be plenty of moments to talk after she felt his touch, after she felt his kiss on her lips.

"I... Do you want..." she stammered. She was so bad at making the first move. Except for their brief time in the truck, it had been forever since she had seduced a man. No matter what anyone said, it wasn't like riding a bike. Just because she had done it a long time ago didn't mean that it would ever come naturally.

She looped her arms around Waylon's waist and laid her head on his chest. His heartbeat was hard and fast under her ear. It was a comfort, as in its rapid cadence she could almost confuse its sound with her own heartbeat.

"Did you call Wyatt to check on Winnie?" he asked, almost as though he wanted to talk about anything other than what their bodies were saying to one another.

She held her breath for a moment, wishing the question could disappear into the thin air between them, but his body tensed with each passing second. Reality pressed in on her, and she finally forced herself to move, looking up at Waylon as she stepped back. Instead of letting her go, as she had expected him to do, he reached down and took hold of her waist.

"How is Winnie?" He frowned. "Is she the reason you're crying? You don't have to be worried about her. She's safe. She'll always be safe."

He really was a good man.

Maybe he would be a good father, too.

A tear slipped down her cheek, but she quickly looked away in an effort to keep him from seeing her cry again. "I called your brother. Winnie is doing just fine. Gwen put her to bed a couple of hours ago. Winnie was a little upset tonight. Apparently, Gwen forgot her favorite doll."

"Do I need to run it over there so she can sleep?"

Christina's knees weakened. He was so sweet and caring.

She wiped away her tears with the back of her hand. "No. Winnie eventually went to bed. She'll be okay, but with everything that's been going on in her life, it's not a huge surprise that she has been regressing lately."

"Regressing?" He frowned.

She nodded. "She's been potty trained for some time, but lately she's been wetting the bed."

His eyes widened. "She's still in diapers?"

Some of the swoon factor receded. Maybe he wasn't the perfect man after all.

"Are you afraid of having a child in diapers?"

He laughed. "No. It's been a while, but I changed more than my fair share of diapers when my parents were working more with the foster care system. It's just that I guess I really hadn't thought about all Winnie must be going through." He nodded. "That kid is a real trouper."

She thought about not speaking her mind, but she'd never really been the kind to sit quietly and let a man take the reins—she was far too strong for that kind of thing. "And putting her through much more…it will only make Winnie's separation from her mother that much harder for her."

He nodded and gave her hips a light squeeze before letting her go. "I know."

No. She should have stayed quiet. The last

thing she wanted to lose right now was the heal-ing power of his touch.

"But you need to do what you think is right. She's your daughter." She reached down and took his hands in hers and interlaced their fin-gers. "Do you know what you want to do?"

"Honestly…" He paused and drew their inter-twined hands up to his mouth and he kissed her fingers. "I have no idea. The only thing I know for sure is that, right now, all I want is you."

He led her down the hallway, and to his old bedroom. His parents hadn't changed it since he'd last lived at home as a kid. There were still posters of early 2000s football player Brett Favre, and a model of the Millennium Falcon hanging from his ceiling. She smiled at his bit of kitschy coolness. It wasn't every day that a man like him would willingly take a woman into a room filled with the memories of his past.

She'd walked by his room a thousand times, but she'd never really paid it any mind and, as he clicked the door shut, for the first time she noticed the *Star Wars* sheets on his bed—complete with Darth Vader on his pillowcase.

"When did you stay here last?" she asked, trying not to think about the lurid, silent promises their bodies were making to one another.

He smiled, and there was a faint redness in his cheeks as though he understood what the place must look like to her. "I have the same exact setup on base. Like it?" he joked. "Though, since I'm older, my action figures have only gotten better." He ran his hands over her curves with a devilish grin.

She giggled. "I had no idea you were this big of a nerd," she teased, relishing the way he gently squeezed her hips.

"Don't get me started on *Star Wars*," he said,

but his tone made it clear it was the last thing on his mind.

"Is there something else you'd rather be doing?" As the words fell from her lips, a feeling of delightful naughtiness whispered through her and made heat rise in her cheeks.

He chuckled, the sound throaty and raw and just as wicked as her words. She loved the erotic sound of his laugh. He wrapped his arms around her waist and pulled her tight against him. So tight she could feel his body's answer to her question.

She reached up to his short, dark hair. It looked sharp but was soft as she ran her fingers through it. It was just like the man it belonged to—high and tight on the outside, but once she really got to know him, he was just a softie.

She had a feeling he let very few people see the man he really was. The thought made her feel even more special and honored to be in his arms and surrounded by his former life.

He lifted her up, and she wrapped her legs around his waist.

"I don't know how we got here. Or why. But I'm so glad we did," he whispered, his hot breath brushing against her lips as he spoke.

The sensation made her shudder.

He closed the gap between them, not waiting for her to answer, and took her lips with his. She ran her tongue over his lips, teasing him with her touch. His lips were strong and giving— So much could be assumed about a man just through his kiss, and from his all she could feel was a passionate future together.

He moved to the bed, but as he walked, his hands slid down to her curves. He cupped his hands over her ass and moaned. She swallowed the sound, relishing its delicious complexity. She rolled her hips slightly, forcing him to hold tighter to her as she pressed against him in all the right ways.

He leaned back slightly to look at her, his eyes heavy with the high of lust and the hunger for more. "What are you trying to do to me?"

"What do you think?" she asked with a playful quirk of the brow.

"Are you sure you want to—"

She pressed her lips against his, the action hard, forcing him to silence. He chuckled, his lips still pressed against hers, and she matched the sound.

He laid her back, their bodies barely parting as he set her down on the bed and moved atop her. Moving down, he laced his kiss over her neck, driving her crazy with desire. When she arched her back, he ran his hands down her front, slowly unbuttoning her shirt as he kissed down her neck and to her collarbone. He pushed back her collar, the dry air brushing against her skin a sharp contrast to the damp trail of his kiss.

She popped open the pearl buttons on his shirt in one swift motion. "Slow," he said with his sexy half grin, the words barely more than a moan. "I want to have you all night long."

Her thighs clenched at the thought. She wasn't sure exactly what her body could handle, but she was willing to test it out. Her mouth moved slowly as she searched for words. She could find only one that her tongue would agree to make. "Please."

She loved the sound of his deep chuckle and the way it reverberated through her, especially through those places where she most yearned for his touch.

He undid the last of her buttons and slipped her shirt off her shoulders. "One thing I've always been trained to do is take orders."

The heat at her core intensified as she realized he wanted her to instruct him on how to touch her. It was definitely outside her comfort zone, but it was what made his request even more desirable. She loved that he pressed her to go further, to trust him and to find pleasure in ways she never had before.

Yet she found it hard to speak her desires as he looked up at her while kissing the soft skin of her belly.

He must have sensed her tentativeness. "Do you like it when I kiss you here?" He pointed at a little freckle on her hip, just above the waist of her jeans. Leaning down, he gently sucked her skin and released it with a kiss.

She smiled. "Yes."

He ran his rough fingers over her lower belly, making the blood rush to the place he had touched. "Do you want me to move lower?"

She nodded, the action slow and deliberate.

He reached down and unbuttoned her pants.

His lips moved over her stomach, and he traced the top of her panty line with his kiss. She squirmed under his touch, aching for more but enjoying each individual kiss as though any one of them could be the last.

If she had a choice, she would live in this place—relishing his kisses and falling deeper and deeper into the euphoria of his touch. She'd never felt anything or anyone better.

He slipped her pants down her legs, caressing each place where her jeans scraped against her flesh. It was a strange sensation, the mix of harsh cotton and the tenderness of his touch. If he wasn't careful, he wouldn't get his turn.

He dropped her pants to the floor, and she sat up, taking him by the flap over his zipper and pulling him closer. His eyes were wide with anticipation and excitement as she slid open his zipper, tooth by tooth. She lavished in the sound of his breath hitching in his throat as she grazed her hand over his responding body. He was hot with want. So hot that her hand was drawn to the heat like a moth to a flame, and just like the moth she couldn't deny there was a certain amount of danger in the choice she was about to make. Yet close on danger's heels was thrill.

But *thrill* didn't fully encompass the feeling she had as she reached inside his open zipper and ran her hand over his length. He groaned as she lowered his pants with her free hand. They fell to the floor with a thump, and he didn't even bother stepping out of them. Instead, he seemed fully consumed in what she was giving him.

She smiled up at him, and their eyes met. It was so sexy when men wore boxers. Especially the kind she could slip her hand into.

"Christina." He whispered her name and he

arched his back slightly, almost in warning of what could happen if she continued.

She considered taking him into her mouth and bringing him to the point of release, yet she wanted more. This was her time to experience all of him, every perfect inch of him.

Slipping her hand out of his boxers, she tugged them down his hips, exposing the dark hair that made a line from his belly and filled in around his ample assets. A giggle escaped her lips as he pulled off his shirt and dropped it to the floor.

"What's so funny?" he asked.

"Nothing."

There was absolutely nothing funny about what was happening between them; rather, the giggle had been an ill-timed attempt to get rid of the nerves that pulsed through her. She wasn't twenty anymore. There were lumps and curves where her skin had once been smooth and inviting, and her breasts were definitely far from the perky peaks they once were.

He pulled back from her touch and stared down at her, almost as though he could sense what she was thinking.

"You know what I like best about you?"

She raised an eyebrow, almost in warning that he'd better get the answer right, as she lay back in bed and rested on her elbows—her breasts taking center stage and looking slightly perkier than they had moments before. In fact, they were almost back to their former glory if they were viewed in just the right light.

"What?"

"I love how confident you are. You're a solid ten anyway, but dang, when you move…"

She smiled. Clearly, he didn't live in her head and hear her thoughts, or he would have known what a self-deprecating and insecure mess she could be. Maybe she was better at faking her confidence than she thought. "What do I move like?" she asked, prompting him to continue his flattery.

"You move like no one else. I guess the best way I can explain it is that when I watch you walk, it's like you are walking only for me." He moved between her legs, pressed her down to the bed and pulled her nipple into his mouth, claiming it.

"Don't you think that's a little selfish?" she asked, trying to ignore the intense rush of feelings that moved through her as her nipple popped out of his mouth.

"Selfish?" He gave her a wicked glance. "I promise you, I'm the least selfish man you will ever know. In fact..." He lowered his hand between her legs and found her, making her gasp. "I think it's better if I just show you how giving I can be."

His fingers moved into her, filling her with

his gentle but confident touch. "Do you like that?"

"Yes," she moaned, "but I want you...all of you..."

He kissed his way up to her lips as his body moved over hers. He slipped inside her. He felt even better than she had dreamed he would. In fact, he fit so well, it made her wonder if their bodies had been made for one another.

As he moved within her, she felt the edge moving closer and closer. From the rhythm of his breath and the way his body was tensing, he was close, too. Before she could say anything, her body defied her and she gave herself completely.

Chapter Fourteen

Sometime in the night, snow had fallen, blanketing the ground and piling up on his window ledge.

Christina's head was on his chest and, as if she could sense him thinking about the chill that awaited them, she snuggled closer.

He'd had to make some hard choices in his life, divorce being right at the top of the list, but nothing was going to be harder than having to decide what he was going to do with this relationship. He had no idea what he was going to do—he'd fallen harder and deeper than he had intended.

Her hair was loose and splayed on his chest. He picked up a strand and wrapped it around his finger. Even her hair was soft, strands of blond silk that were just as strong as the woman they belonged to. Everything about her, even down to her pit bull–like stare when she had first met him, was perfect.

He gently ran his fingers through her hair, careful not to wake her up, but he just needed to touch her. They had only a few days until he had to get back on a jet and fly all the way across the country.

It struck him how everything had moved so fast. It was crazy to think they had been strangers only a matter of days before, and now he was thinking about changing his life for the woman in his arms. Even though it had been quick, he wasn't afraid—and that thought was what scared him the most.

He wasn't new to the world of falling in love.

He should have been more controlled, more metered in his approach, but there was just something about Christina that made him throw caution to the wayside. Hopefully he wouldn't come to regret his reckless behavior—he wasn't sure that he could handle another Bell woman breaking his heart. He could only spend so many years in the military.

Waylon's body tightened when he heard the thump of footfalls in the hallway. After a brief knock on the door, the doorknob twisted. He moved quickly to cover their entangled bodies with a blanket, and if he'd been a little younger, he would have pulled it all the way over his head, but there was no hiding the facts.

Wyatt barged in, and though it was early, he must have already been at work, as he was decked out in his uniform. "Get your a—" Wyatt stopped midword as he stared at them. "Dude." His mouth opened and closed for a

minute, then he turned away and stepped back
into the hall, closing the door behind him.

Great. Waylon sighed. Now his morning
would be filled with knowing glances and his
brother's hounding.

There was a light tap on the door, as though
Wyatt was going for strike two.

"What?" Waylon grumbled.

"Um," Wyatt started. "We need to talk. I got
some news. Take your time."

Waylon snorted. Like he needed his brother's
permission or direction to do anything, especially when it came to women. Admittedly,
though, he couldn't deny the fact there were
times, just like this one, when he wasn't exactly sure what his next move should be. Talking to his brother about his situation sounded
just about as fun as going to the dentist. He
and Wyatt could talk about a lot, but the topic
of Christina somehow seemed off-limits. On

the other hand, Wyatt knew her better than Waylon did.

He moved from the bed, pulling himself out from Christina's hold ever so slowly to keep from waking her. It was strange how cold the room felt now that he wasn't wrapped in her arms. He'd spent hundreds of training hours covered in mud and lying in stagnant swamp water, and in those moments he had thought he was cold, but it was nothing in comparison to the chill he felt without her against him.

He looked back at her as he slipped into his clothes.

She stirred slightly and moaned, as though she was protesting his absence in her sleep. Her moan made him think of the way she had sounded and looked under him last night. The thought made his body stir, and he forced himself to look away. There wasn't time to do the things he wanted to do to her now, but given another chance, he would ravage her and make her purr like the sexy lioness she was.

He chuckled at the thought. He would give just about anything to have enough time to make her go from a purr to a roar.

Wyatt, standing in the living room, turned toward him as he made his way down the hall. Waylon sighed as he imagined all the things his brother was probably going to say.

"Say whatever it is you're dying to say," Waylon said, motioning down the hallway toward his room.

"Hmm?" his brother asked, a mischievous grin on his face. "What do you want me to say?"

Waylon snorted. "Nothing. Nothing at all."

"I get one, then I'll leave it alone," Wyatt said. "Just don't hurt her. She's a good one. She may come off like she's as tough as nails, but she's not. She has been through a lot, especially with everything going on with her sister. Gwen and she are good friends, but even Gwen may not be able to save her if you decide to go on and break her heart."

"I have no intention of breaking her heart."

"Intention or no intention, if you've got her in your bed, you are only setting her up to fall."

He couldn't deny the fact his brother was right.

Wyatt gave him *that* look, the look that he'd given him every time he'd been in trouble as a kid. "There's no good way out of the hole you've started to dig with her."

There was a good way out, but not one he would dare whisper. The second he started to talk about something more, something like a future, was the moment everything had a way of going wrong.

"I wouldn't call what we are doing digging a hole."

"Then what exactly would you call it? You are going to love her and leave her. Just like you did with Alli, and we all know exactly how well that turned out." Wyatt motioned around them, like Alli was some kind of omnipresent being.

"Are you kidding me?" Waylon tried to control his anger. He couldn't be mad at his brother for warning him—he was just stepping up to the plate and making sure no one got hurt. In a way, his brother might be far wiser than him. Then again, Wyatt didn't have a right to try to lay the blame of everything that had happened with Alli on Waylon. "None of this is my fault. Alli is a big girl. What she does or doesn't do is on her."

"I know. You're right." Wyatt let out a long breath as he pinched the bridge of his nose. "It's just…"

"You don't want anyone to get hurt," Waylon

said, finishing his sentence. "Believe me when I say I don't want her to get hurt, either."

"If that was true, you wouldn't have—"

"Stop," Waylon said, putting his hands up in surrender. "You said you only got *one*. One was enough. You're just going to have to trust me when I say I only want the best for Christina, and I care for her."

Wyatt nodded. "Good. Just as long as we know where we both stand. I don't want to be the one stuck here holding the emotional baggage you leave behind. Again."

"Enough," Waylon grumbled. "If you just woke me up to have a talk, I'm going back to bed, and to her."

"Wait," Wyatt said, stopping him as he started to walk out of the room. "I'm sorry. Seriously, man, I guess that—" he motioned down the hall "—just caught me by surprise. I'll be okay with it, I swear. You know, Gwen and I...you know how we've been over the years. I guess maybe I don't have any room to judge how you go about your love life."

At least his brother had stepped back into the land of the reasonable. "Thanks, man. You know how it can be. Sometimes things just happen."

"You mean like *love*?" Wyatt scanned him, looking at Waylon like he was trying to find some twitch that would give his true feelings away.

Did he love Christina? There were definitely things he really liked about her—her personality, how smart and driven she was, how her hair fell down her back and caressed her skin. She was so dang sexy. Yet she could set his teeth on edge in a matter of seconds when she wanted—especially when they talked about Winnie.

If he made the decision to take Winnie with him back to Fort Bragg... Well, whatever fondness Christina felt for him would probably disappear more quickly than his independence. Yet if he left the girl with them at the ranch, she would undoubtedly come to resent him and his inability to be a father.

The old adage "Danged if you do, and danged if you don't" came to mind.

"Why did you wake me up?" Waylon asked, mostly out of a desire to avoid answering Wyatt's prying question.

Wyatt smirked. "I thought you'd like to know we got a hit on the ring that went missing from the lockbox. Apparently, someone pawned it to a place in Flintlock last night."

"There have to be at least four pawnshops between here and there," Waylon said, trying to recall the town just south of them that was little more than a speck on a map.

Wyatt nodded. "Maybe Alli thought she was far enough outside our range."

"It's still in Flathead County. She had to know you would get a call."

"Unless she thought she could get away with taking the ring without anyone noticing it was missing."

"Did you go through the documents in the box? Was there anything missing from those? Something that Christina might not have noticed?"

Wyatt shrugged. "Lyle and my team went through the room. It had been rifled through, but I wouldn't know if something else was taken. When I talked to Christina, not even she knew exactly what was in that box."

"Don't you think it would hold official documents? Maybe something like Winnie's birth certificate? Or her Social Security card. Did you find any of those kinds of things for Winnie?"

"There were only a few deeds and a car title."

Waylon motioned toward the room. "I bet you a hundred bucks if you go back in there and look in that box, that stuff is missing."

They made their way down the hall to Winnie's room. Someone had picked it up, as the little bed was made and all the toys were back in place. Wyatt walked to the closet and pulled the safe off the shelf. He opened it and shuffled through the papers. After a moment he looked up. "How did you know they wouldn't be in here?"

"I don't know. I guess ever since I found out about Winnie, I've just been thinking about all the things I would need for her. If Alli is going to take her, she's going to need those documents—especially if she wanted to take her over the border. Does Winnie have a passport?"

The color drained from Wyatt's face.

"Let me guess. It's missing, too?"

Wyatt nodded. "But Gwen would never let Alli get her hands on the girl. Don't worry."

"If she gets her hands on Winnie and makes it over the border, we'll never get her back. Under no circumstances is Gwen to leave Winnie alone. Got it?"

"She knows. Don't worry," Wyatt said. "If you think she wouldn't do everything in her power to keep Winnie safe, you're crazy. She loves that girl—maybe even more than you do. She's known Winnie since the day she was born."

His brother's words stung, but Waylon didn't have time to dwell on it. If anything, he would just have to get used to everyone judging him for a mistake he hadn't known he'd made. If that was the price of having his daughter in his life, then it was a price he was willing to pay.

There was a knock on the door. Christina stood there, looking in at them. She was dressed and her hair was pulled back into a messy bun, but the haze of sleep was still in her eyes. "What are you guys doing in here?" she asked, her voice sounding as groggy as she looked.

"I'll explain it on the drive," Waylon said, taking her by the hand and leading her to the truck.

"On the drive? Where are we going?" she asked.

At least she had finally come to trust him and the fact he wasn't out to hurt her or his family. Unfortunately, Wyatt was right. In a couple of days, that was exactly what he'd be doing—hurting the woman he cared about.

There was no doubt in his mind that they shouldn't have slept together, but when her fingers laced between his, his heart told him he had made the right choice last night. Spending the night holding her in his arms, her head on his chest, had been the best night he'd had in a long time. It had been something so beyond a one-night stand, even though he had the impression that neither of them intended to make it more than just that.

It was strange how things could change in just a few seconds when they chose to open up their hearts. There would be no going back to the way things had been between them. For the rest of time, regardless of what the future brought, they would have the special bond that only lovers were blessed to experience.

Wyatt walked over to his patrol unit. "I'll lead the way. Try to keep up."

Waylon answered with a nod as he helped Christina into her truck.

"If you're going to drag me around, I'm going to need a cup of coffee. Especially after last night," she said, an air of satisfaction in her tone.

"If we had time, I'd make you a cup, but we need to head out."

"Okay, then you'll at least have to tell me where we're going."

"We're heading to Flintlock," he said. "We got a hit on your grandmother's ring. Apparently, someone pawned it."

Her early-morning smile disappeared, and he instantly wished he hadn't told her, but there was no avoiding the reality that last night, and what had happened between them, was officially over—no matter how badly he wished he could scoop her up in his arms and carry her back to his bed, *Star Wars* sheets and all.

He laughed as he thought about how often in high school he'd dreamed of bringing a girl back to his room, and how it had never happened. Yet now that he hadn't been looking, it had come to fruition.

He slipped into the driver's seat and followed Wyatt out onto the highway that bridged the gap between the two towns.

Some of the ease they'd had with each other before had disappeared now that they were alone in the truck. It was like she also realized their time was coming to an end. She laid her hand between them on the bench seat, palm up. He almost reached for it, but as he started to move, she closed her fingers and pulled her hand back, balling it up in her lap.

"Did your brother have anything to say about finding us in bed together?" she asked, her words as tight as her fist.

"Yeah, he definitely had an opinion."

"One you care to share?" She glanced over at him.

He put his hand atop her fist in an attempt to stop her from closing off more and more to him. He couldn't handle being back on the outs with her. As long as he was here, he wanted things to be as they had been last night—open and filled with laughter. Yet he couldn't deny the fact that some desires couldn't survive in the glaring light of day—they were burned away by the harsh reality of their lives like shadows in the sun.

She didn't loosen her fist, so he drew his hand away. She didn't want him. Or at least, just like him, she was realizing all the reasons she had to close herself off and protect her core. That was what it was—a protective measure. He would be smart to follow her lead.

"You know Wyatt," he said, gripping the wheel hard with both hands. "He thinks just 'cause he's the oldest, he has all the right answers."

"What does he think the right answer is when it comes to you and me?"

He shrugged. "He's not always right."

"So he thinks it's a bad idea?"

Waylon wasn't sure what he wanted to talk about less—her grandmother's ring being

pawned or the state of their relationship—or
rather, the *lack of,* based on the state of things.
Both topics seemed to make her tighten up.
He would give anything just to make her easy
smile return.

"Some of the greatest things in life have
started out as bad ideas."

She laughed. The sound was warm, and he
found it impossible not to laugh with her and
mimic her intoxicating sound. What it would
have been like to hear that sound every day.

"You and I, we've done too much living to
believe in some idealistic notion that the heart
always leads us in the right direction. The heart
is a fickle and mercurial thing."

"Are you saying you regret what happened
last night?" He felt almost at a loss at the
fact that he wasn't the one controlling the conversation and that she was taking the lead in

what would undoubtedly be her attempt to push him away.

She looked down at her fingers. "I know, as I'm sure that you do, too, that last night…it was great, but…"

"But you don't want anything more from me?" he said, trying to steel himself against the stinging truth of her words.

"That's not it…" She gazed over at him, and there was the faintest hint of tears in her eyes. "It's just…this…it can't be. Our lives are too different. You don't belong here anymore. You have the world at your fingertips. If I asked you to stay, or to come back to me, I'd be asking you to give up the world. I'd never ask that of you."

"Then why don't you come with me?" The words flew out of his mouth without him really thinking about what he was asking her to do.

"It's not as simple as that. With everything going on with Winnie and with the ranch…

your mom needs me here. My life is here. Besides, if I went with you, what would there be for me to do?"

"We could be together. What's more important than that?" The pain that pierced him made its way into his voice, but he didn't have the power to keep it in check.

"Waylon, you don't know me well…"

"I know you better than you want to admit," he argued. "I know the face you make when you are truly happy, and the face you make when you think someone you love is in danger." A tiny smile lighted over his lips as he thought about her standing on the front porch of the main house as he'd landed in the Black Hawk. "And I know how much you try to control every situation in order to keep yourself from getting hurt."

She sucked in a breath as though he'd struck a chord. "You're right, Waylon. I don't want to get hurt. And I don't want to get hurt a year from now. Let's just tell it like it is. I mean, think about it. What would I do while you're off working every day? What would there be for me at Fort Bragg? And what about Winnie? You can't think that raising her on a military base would be better than raising her on the ranch."

"Plenty of kids grow up on the bases."

"Sure, they move from one place to another. They make friends, and then those friends leave."

"They grow up strong," he argued. "They grow up knowing that the only thing they can really rely on is themselves and their family."

"Don't you think that Winnie can grow up just as strong here? Here she would have stability—and that's something that has been desperately lacking in her life since her mother disappeared."

This time, she was the one who was right. Winnie deserved to have the best in life. And maybe Christina had a clearer view of exactly what that was.

Christina reached over to him, but he wouldn't let go of the steering wheel. No. He couldn't let her see his pain. He was too strong for that. He'd already opened himself up too much. He'd been an idiot, and it had been too long since he'd been down this road. He'd almost forgotten how much it hurt to have himself torn apart.

There was no possibility of a future. All he could ever have with her was a friendship and thoughts of what might have been if their lives had made their dreams possible.

He was relieved when they passed the log sign that said Welcome to Flintlock. At least he could get out of the car and away from the conversation that would only lead him farther down a path he didn't want to travel.

Flintlock was made up of a railroad track, a gas station, two bars, two churches, a pawnshop and a bank—it was little more than a place in which a road-worn traveler could make a pit stop before getting back on their way. Waylon followed Wyatt into the pawnshop's parking lot.

The pawnshop was a squat, square building with shake siding that had little chinks in it where pieces had rotted out and fallen to the ground. The place's windows were dark, but the Open sign was on, making Wyatt wonder if the windows had been tinted in an effort to mask whatever nefarious deeds normally happened inside.

He hated the place before he even stepped out of the truck, but he reminded himself that maybe it wasn't as bad as he assumed—at least they had called in a tip. The owner or an employee could have simply bought the ring or turned Alli away and never reported anything.

It would have been easier for them not having to deal with the police.

At a place like this, probably the last thing they wanted was police to come sniffing around.

Waylon stepped out of the truck, thankful for an escape from their conversation. Christina shook her head as she got out and followed him over to Wyatt, who was waiting beside his car.

"A guy named Herb called in the tip. He should still be working. He's a nice guy, been in this game a long time, but you want to be careful. In fact, I'll just take the lead on this one. Cool?"

Waylon nodded, but the last thing he wanted to do was play second fiddle to his brother. Yet this wasn't his investigation—or his jurisdiction.

Most of the lights were off in the pawnshop, and it was barely bright enough for them to navigate through the racks of old guitars and outdated DVDs. The place beckoned of lost paths and sadness.

An old man sat behind a long glass counter in the back of the store. Inside the display case was a collection of handguns and expensive jewelry. It struck Waylon as funny that the guns didn't really seem out of place next to the pawned wedding bands—rings that had likely been sold by those who'd had their hearts destroyed.

Or maybe that was just his pain talking.

"How y'all doin'?" the guy behind the counter asked as he stood up from the bar stool. He had gray hair and a barrel chest, and though he was crooked from the ravages of age, he stood at least six and a half feet tall. Beneath him, the little wooden bar stool teetered as if it feared the man would sit down on it again.

"Doin' real well, Herb. We appreciate you

giving us a call." Wyatt shook the man's hand and motioned toward them. "This is my brother and his girlfriend, Christina. Actually, it was Christina's ring that was reported stolen."

Waylon tried to pretend he didn't notice the look of surprise on Christina's face at Wyatt's introduction.

"Ah," the guy said, looking her up and down. "That ring is almost as pretty as its owner." He whistled through the gap in his front teeth.

Christina looked away, suddenly passive in the presence of the man.

"Did you purchase the ring, Herb?" Waylon asked, trying to help Christina escape what could become the man's full-court press.

Herb reached under the counter and pulled out a receipt book, the kind that most stores didn't seem to use anymore, but that were common in parts of the world where internet service and sometimes even cell phones were a luxury.

"The guy was selling quite a few things. A few pieces of artwork and two rings." He tapped the receipt as he spoke.

"The guy? The person who came in and sold you the ring was a guy?" Christina asked, shock filling her voice.

Waylon was just as surprised as Christina. There had been no talk of any man in Alli's life except William Poe. Was it possible that William had been the man here selling things? It seemed like a long shot. William would never stick his neck out, not now when so many people were watching him.

"What did the man look like? Was he a business type?" Wyatt asked. He must have been thinking about William as well.

Herb waved him off. "No. The guy was hefty, big belly, and long, greasy hair. Nice, liked to chat, but I have a feeling it's because he spends a lot of time on his own. If I remember correct, he mighta said he was a trucker."

"A trucker?" Waylon glanced over at his brother, who gave him a small, almost imperceptible nod. "By chance did you manage to catch the guy's name?"

Herb shook his head. "Can't remember the guy's name off the top of my head, but I got a little card with some information."

Waylon had to reach deep as he tried to recall the name of the trucker they'd met at the pullout where Alli's car was found. "Does the name Daryl sound familiar?"

Was it possible the man was more involved than he had let them believe? Had he been helping Alli ever since he found her along the side of the road? Or that he had known Alli even before he'd picked her up and they had been following all the wrong leads?

A thousand questions and even more possibilities came to mind—followed by a litany of mistakes Waylon had made. He had been so wrapped up in uncovering the secrets within his family and following his heart's wants that he had managed to miss a clue that had literally stared him in the face.

On the other hand, the guy hadn't given them much to work with, nor had he given them any indication he was more involved with Alli than he had told them. It was possible that the man who'd brought in the jewelry and art wasn't the same guy they had met on the side of the road. Or maybe Alli had set them up and she wanted them to chase their tails.

Herb reached under his counter and took out an old metal box. Opening it up, he frowned at its contents for a moment before turning the box around for them to see. Inside the box was a gold band with a large cushion-cut diamond flanked by sapphires. It was a beautiful ring;

Christina's description had barely done it justice. Yet, as with so many things in life, being told something was a poor replacement for living it.

He glanced over at Christina. She had her hands clapped over her mouth. "How much?" she asked from between her fingers. "At least tell me how much you gave the guy for my grandmother's ring."

"I paid five hundred, but you guys don't owe me a dime. I barely gave him anything for the paintings." Herb pointed to two paintings leaning against the back wall behind the counter. They had dabs of paint here and there and looked like something Winnie could have made. "The guy who came in seemed to know a lot about the ring, but he barely knew anything about art. Those paintings are worth ten of those rings. They're originals. I think I'm gonna go ahead and send them off to Sotheby's for auction."

Waylon stared at the paintings. One had a red glob surrounded by sharp black lines, and he could tell exactly why the seller had thought the thing was worthless. When it came to art, he didn't understand why someone would be willing to pay hundreds of thousands of dollars for something they put on their wall and could just say they owned—not when they could spend that same money on living their lives and experiencing the world.

"Did he mention where he got the paintings?" Waylon asked.

"You know how it is," Herb said with a shrug. "Some people want to tell you their whole life story, but the ones you want to hear are the ones that you don't get. You're lucky I even managed to get his name and address. He wanted to dicker over that as well. I wouldn't be surprised if the information he gave me ends up being phony." Herb reached into the metal box and handed the ring and the card beneath it over to Waylon.

Waylon stared at the name: Jeb Bush. Herb was right; the guy had definitely given him a fake name.

"Wyatt, you ever heard of Running Deer Lane?" Waylon moved the card over so his brother could see it.

Wyatt took the card and threw it down on the counter. "Yeah. The guy was full of crap, there's no such address. Did you ask to see his driver's license?"

"No," Herb said, shaking his head. "But I did manage to get his license plate number before he drove off."

Finally, they had a tie to Alli—hopefully they could get to her before anyone got hurt.

Chapter Fifteen

Five hundred dollars. Not only had her sister murdered, but she had also stolen from her and pawned a symbol of what little was left of their family, and she had done it for five hundred dollars. A lump rose in Christina's throat, and though she shouldn't have let this hurt, she couldn't help but succumb to the lashes of her sister's actions.

Perhaps Alli *was* on drugs. It wasn't the first time the thought had crossed her mind, but she always tried to have a little bit more faith that her sister would make better decisions. Looking back, though, she felt like a fool. Maybe if she just started thinking the worst of her sister, then she would no longer be surprised or agonize when Alli did the things she did.

Christina twisted her grandmother's ring around her finger. It was a little tight for the ring finger on her right hand, but until she could put it back in its box and get it tucked away somewhere Alli would never find it, she could think of no better place than her own hand to keep it safe. It was funny. She could protect things by keeping them close to her—everything except her feelings.

Wyatt was across the parking lot, running the plates in his squad car. Tiny, almost ash-like snowflakes fell from the sky and, as the wind picked up, scattered like secrets throughout the small town.

The thought of secrets and the power they wielded made Christina rub the ring finger on her left hand. Her sister's secrets had nearly cost them everything—even a chance at a future.

She glanced down at the ring as a snowflake drifted down and melted on the surface of the diamond. She thought about slipping the ring off and putting it on her other hand, feeling the weight of the engagement ring and what it had the potential to mean—loyalty, fidelity, love, trust and being loved forever by the man of her dreams.

She glanced up and caught Waylon looking at her.

"You all right?" Waylon asked, nodding toward her hand. "I'm sure she was just desperate. You know, selling the ring and all. And when people are desperate, they do desperate things."

"I know. It's just that..." As she looked over at him, her thoughts moved to him between her legs, looking down at her with something that was well beyond lust—and a lot like love.

"Just what?" Waylon moved closer but stopped short, almost as though he wasn't sure whether or not he should come any closer.

"I'm not a wild dog. I'm not going to bite," she said, but even as she spoke, she knew it had come off just like a snip. The look on his face confirmed her fears. "Sorry, I'm not upset with you. It's just…well, I wish Alli would just stop doing what she's doing. It's almost like everything she is doing and trying, she is doing to hurt me and her daughter. I just can't figure out what I did to her that would make her want to hurt me like this. All I ever did was try to help her. I came here for her. I agreed to take her daughter. All I ever wanted to do was be the best sister I could. We were all we had for each other…" She tried to continue, but she couldn't get any more words past the lump in her throat.

Waylon rushed over to her and pulled her into his arms. His chin rested on her head as she let him hold her. It was all too much. Being with him. Losing Alli. Fighting for Winnie. Being strong…all the time. For this moment, and just this moment, she let herself be weak.

Sometimes the soul needed a moment of weakness so a person could really appreciate its moments of strength.

Waylon rubbed her back as she laid her head against his chest. It felt so good to be held by him. Being with him was what she hadn't known she was missing, but now that she realized it, she couldn't imagine him being anywhere else but with her. She didn't have a clue what she was going to do with herself once he was gone. Things could never go back to the way they were—and once again, her life would be in flux.

When would life just *be*? Why did everything

have to be a fight? Why couldn't she just have what she wanted—a future with him?

She sucked in a long breath as she tried to take back control over her feelings. Right now, she couldn't dwell on them. There was too much to lose and too much at risk to start wallowing in a land of what-ifs.

She pulled out of Waylon's arms just as Wyatt stepped out of his car and made his way over to them.

"Everything all right, Christina?" Wyatt asked, his face filled with concern.

Of course he would be worried. As long as they had known each other, he had never seen her fall into the arms of a man in a moment of need, but if the events of late had taught her anything, it was that anything was possible— even the things she feared the most.

"I'm fine," she said, attempting to swallow

back the lump in her throat. "What did you find out?"

"We ran the plate numbers and it looks like the truck does, in fact, belong to Daryl," Wyatt said. "You guys want to run over there and question him with me?"

"Let's go. If Daryl knows where we can find Alli, maybe we can have her in custody by this afternoon."

"And you can hit the road?" Even Christina heard the acidic tone as it burned away any softness from her voice.

Waylon reached toward her, but she stepped away from his touch. His eyes widened, and he looked shocked and confused by her refusal. Instead of falling victim to that look—the look that said he needed her—she forced herself to turn away.

Wyatt's phone rang, and he motioned for

them to hold on for a second as he answered it. "What's up, babe?"

A fast and erratic woman's voice came through the speaker—Christina assumed it was Gwen, but she couldn't quite make out the words. Wyatt's face blanched as she spoke.

"No…" he said, almost on an exhale. "It's okay. It's going to be okay. I'm sure she's okay. How did she get her?"

Get who? She glanced over at Waylon, and his mouth was pinched and a storm raged in his eyes. "He's not talking about Winnie, is he?" she asked, though she already knew the answer.

Wyatt leaned against the front of the pawnshop and ran his hand over his face.

"Don't worry. I'm on my way. We'll get her back. Come hell or high water, we will find Winnie." Wyatt looked up at Christina, and this time there were tears in his eyes—tears that made her entire body go numb.

WINNIE WAS GONE, stolen from Gwen's care. One minute she had been safe at home, and the next she had simply disappeared.

Waylon had promised Christina they would keep her safe, yet he had let Alli take her—and if anything happened to her, he wasn't sure he would be able to live with himself. He'd known he was a father for a day, and as already culpable in letting his little girl fall into the wrong hands.

Christina had been right in thinking him incapable of being someone's father. In fact, he shouldn't have even had the right to call Winnie his daughter. He didn't deserve something that good in his life.

Wyatt had gone straight over to his house to get Gwen, who had grown more and more hysterical over the phone. He could imagine how bad she was feeling right now, but no matter how badly he wanted to push the blame on her

for what had happened, he couldn't blame anyone but himself. He shouldn't have let Winnie
leave his side, yet instead of taking her under
his wing, he had let others care for her.

He glanced over at Christina as he drove toward the address Wyatt had given them for the
trucker. Christina's face was steely, and she was
staring out of the truck with such intensity he
wondered how the glass wasn't melting. She
was being strong—and that was exactly what
he needed to be as well.

This couldn't be about emotions. From now
until Winnie was found, they could only focus
on the things they could control. They should
only have one objective—to get Winnie back.
After that, he and Christina could focus on
Alli and perhaps talk about a future, but as it
was, there was no way he could think about the
needs of his heart. Not when it was utterly bro-

ken at the thoughts of what his daughter was possibly facing.

"Alli would never do anything to hurt Winnie," he said, trying to not only make Christina feel better but to reassure himself as well.

Christina didn't even bat an eyelash. "Sure. Of course she wouldn't." Her voice was flat and emotionless.

He could handle her display of emotions so much better than her arctic front.

"I'm so sorry about this, Christina," he said, trying again to comfort her.

This time she glanced over at him, and the chill in her voice had overtaken her gaze as well. Some of the iciness penetrated his core and seeped into his heart.

"I told you this was going to happen. I told you Winnie wasn't safe. We should have brought her with us."

He didn't want to bring up the fact that they

had been busy doing other things—things that would have never happened if they had a child with them—but he stopped himself. She hated him. Bringing up anything that had happened between them would be disastrous. In truth, he didn't blame her. He hated himself just as much for what he had allowed, albeit passively, to happen to Winnie.

"You're right," he said, submitting himself to her derision. He deserved whatever punishment she wished to deliver. "I never should have let her out of my sight. No matter how bad you are feeling right now, just know I'm feeling a thousand times worse. I know this is my fault. I was stupid to think Gwen could have kept her safe. Alli knows too much about the ranch and Gwen's movements. If I'd trusted my gut, none of this would have ever happened."

"Maybe everything…everything has been a huge mistake."

"That's not what I meant," he said. "You have to know that's not what I meant. What you and I shared last night—"

"Was stupid," she said, finishing his sentence. "If we just hadn't lost focus, none of this would have happened." She glared over at him, and her lip twitched with anger. "I told you almost the second you set foot on the ranch that Winnie was, and will always be, my primary concern. I am her guardian. You coming here put her at risk."

"My coming here has nothing to do with your sister coming back and kidnapping Winnie. And what happened between you and me wasn't stupid. You can't tell me you didn't enjoy it just as much as me. You are hurt and angry. I get that. But don't forget we're on the same side."

"We are not on the same side. We've never been on the same side."

She was pissed, and she had every right to be, but she was wrong. Yet trying to argue with her would be futile.

He could only watch and listen as she attempted to shatter the bond they shared.

He'd always been one to be the hero, to save those who needed saving and help people through their darkest moments, but he hadn't had a clue that when he came back to Montana he would be facing his own personal version of hell.

All he could do was hope that he would be able to save Winnie. If she got hurt, or if Alli made some stupid decision, he would let his rage take over. He would no longer be a hero—he would be a man thirsty for vengeance.

"Winnie is going to be fine. They are going to start searching the ranch. For all we know she's still there. Safe and sound." He said it aloud, but the words sounded muted, like they were coming from the other side of the glass.

Christina said something under her breath he was glad he couldn't hear.

They barreled down a dirt road just on the edge of the county line. A trailer sat at the end of the drive, its roof was covered in bits of tarp and one of its front windows was held together with duct tape. Even by Montana standards, the place was a crap hole.

For a passing moment, he wondered if Alli had brought Winnie to this rat-infested place. He had to brush the thought aside. He needed to treat this case like it was just any other missing person—and not his daughter. If he let this be personal, he wouldn't have the control required to do the job that needed to be done.

He pulled in behind the big rig parked beside the trailer. Now that they were close, he could see the place listed a bit to the left, almost as though it, too, was ashamed of the wreckage it had become.

He got out and came around to open Christina's door for her. It was a feeble gesture, but hopefully she would see it as the peace offering he intended.

"If you think you're going to tell me to sit here and wait, you've got another think coming," she said, pushing out of the truck. She didn't even look back as she made her way toward the front door of the house.

He rushed to catch up. "I'm not the kind of guy who would ever ask you to stand by and watch as a man does the work. Do you really think I'm a jerk?" He instantly wished he could reel the words back in. He wasn't sure he wanted her to answer.

She snorted slightly, but then as she turned to face him, she stopped. "You are not a jerk." She stared at him for a moment, and some of the iciness of her gaze melted away. "You just need to do everything in your power to save my niece." She turned back away and took the steps leading to the door two at a time. She knocked on the door; the sound was hollow and echoed through the house as though it was made of nothing more than cheap particleboard and spackle.

The cheap blinds rattled, as someone must have looked out at them from the living room.

"Daryl! Daryl Bucket?" she yelled. "We know you're inside. Answer the damned door!"

Waylon could hear heavy footfalls as the man made his way down the hall. Daryl opened the door just far enough that Waylon could see one of the man's eyes. His cheeks were covered with a day's worth of stubble, and from what Waylon could make out from the array of stains on the man's white shirt, he must have eaten a week's worth of Cheetos and used his T-shirt as a rag.

"What the hell do you want?" Daryl's voice was hoarse from lack of use and, from the tarry scent of the trailer, a hefty addiction to cigarettes.

"I'm not sure if you recognize us, but—" Waylon started.

"I know who you are. Why are you here?"

"We just wanted to ask you a few questions. No big deal, man, but we would appreciate your help," he said, trying to act as chummy as possible, though every cell of his being wanted to reach through the crack in the door, take the man by the throat and make him answer every one of his questions to his satisfaction.

"Hmm." Daryl ran his fingers through his greasy hair. "All right, army boy. You can come in, but I got stuff to do." He opened the door, and in his right hand once again was his trusty bat.

They followed him down the narrow hall. It was covered in old grainy photographs of green-clad marines posing with antiquated tanks and helicopters in what looked like the jungles of Vietnam. Daryl rubbed the bat on the wall, making an unsettling sound as he walked into the living room.

He flopped down in a threadbare recliner and set his bat across his lap as he looked up at them.

Waylon couldn't help but wonder what kind of life the old marine had lived that he thought he always needed a weapon. Though they were in different branches, he had a certain level of understanding of the world outside the United States.

When a person had experienced the brutal reality of combat, there was no going back to a life in which they could ever really feel at peace. Safety was merely an illusion—an illusion he had perpetuated by telling Christina that Winnie was safe. How could he have been so stupid? How could he have looked past the lessons that had been drilled into him—the lesson that the only person he could really trust was himself?

He stared at Daryl and his bat. The only real difference between him and that man was Waylon wasn't carrying a bat—they were both equally a mess by the hand life had dealt them. Daryl just had the luxury of trying to forget.

"What kind of *stuff* do you have to do?" Christina asked, nearly spitting the words.

"That ain't none of your business, eh," the guy said, his warm Canadian accent in juxtaposition to his harsh words.

"I know, man. We don't have any business coming here and buggin' you when you got places to be. I get it." Waylon tried his best to overcome the jagged edge of Christina's tone. "We just had reason to believe that you might know a thing or two that could come in handy in helping us."

"Helping you all with what?" Daryl asked.

"We heard a little rumor that you sold some things to a pawnshop last night. Is that correct?"

Daryl didn't say anything; he simply spun the bat around in his hands.

"There's nothing wrong with pawning a couple of things to make an extra buck here or there," Waylon said. "Heaven knows I've needed a couple extra bucks now and then."

"You're still active. You don't got a clue. You would have thought my going to fight for your country woulda proved my allegiance and set me up for retirement, but that ain't happening. Ya know?"

"What do you mean? Isn't the VA treating you right?"

Daryl twisted the bat again. "As a former Canadian, I was only ever eligible for jobs that didn't require security clearance. You know what I mean, eh? The only good thing to come of my enlistment was my citizenship, but now that I been in the States most of my life and saw what a mess your political system is, I may just have to turn around and go back up north." He laughed.

"I wouldn't blame you, man." Waylon stepped over to the window and turned slightly so the guy could be a little more comfortable. "So you sold the ring. No problem." He glanced over at Christina, who slipped her hands behind her back in an effort to hide the ring from view.

"Then what's the problem?" Daryl asked. "What brought you all the way up here to my door?"

"We were just wondering where exactly you got that ring. Do you remember?"

"Did she steal it?" Daryl asked, staring at the bat in his hands.

"She did," Waylon said. "Do you know where we can find her?"

Daryl shook his head. "Truth be told, I don't even know how she found me, but she musta searched my name or something. Anyways, she showed up on my doorstep in what I now gotta assume was a stolen car and asked me if I could help her out by taking a few things off her hands. In my defense, she didn't tell me they were stolen. I wouldn't have bought none of it if I'd known for sure they were hot."

"Yet you gave the pawnshop owner a fake name and address when you sold him the stuff?"

Daryl twitched. "Is someone on the way here to arrest me? I swear I didn't know for sure. I just had a feeling. And I needed the money. She gave everything to me for a real good price. It was a good investment. That was all," he rambled.

"You're not in trouble, and the cops don't have a reason to come on out here and bother you, if you give us the answers we need."

"Look, army boy, I really would love to help you all, but I don't know nothing." He glanced back down at the bat in his hands, but not before Waylon noticed the faint redness in his cheeks—a color that told him there was far more to the story than the man wanted to admit, especially in front of a woman.

Waylon turned to Christina. "You mind if I talk to him alone for a minute?" He felt bad for asking, especially since he had just told her he wasn't the kind of guy to push a woman to the side, but there was no getting around it with the retired marine.

Christina opened her mouth to say something but stopped as she looked at him. "Daryl, do you have anything to drink in the kitchen?"

He pointed farther down the hall. "There's some coffee from earlier this morning. And there might be a few beers left in the fridge. Help yourself."

Christina frowned but made her way out of the room and toward the kitchen.

Waylon turned back to Daryl. "So was she good? You know, the girl who you bought the ring from."

Daryl jerked as he looked up at him, and the way the man's mouth opened and closed—like he was searching for air—told Waylon he'd hit the nail on the head.

"A man has needs. You're fine," Waylon said with a shrug. "Not to mention that Alli is a beautiful woman. I don't blame you for making a move on her." Actually, he hated the thought of the things Alli had done and continued to do, but that was hardly the man's fault.

"Alli? Who's Alli?" Daryl frowned. "She said her name was Sharon. At least I think that's what she said."

It didn't surprise him that Alli would have given the guy a fake name. There seemed to be a lot of that going around. In fact, it might even have been where Daryl had gotten the idea, but he didn't bother to ask.

"What did Sharon look like?"

"I told you before, dark haired, about five foot six, skinny—though she looked like she'd lost weight from the last time I'd saw her. It's another reason I wanted to help her out."

Daryl could try to make it sound like he was helping the woman out of the goodness of his heart, but he'd already admitted to letting her exchange sex for favors and profiting from a stolen item. He was no saint.

"Is there anything else you can tell me?"

Daryl shook his head.

"You saw her naked. Did she have any kind of birthmarks? Tattoos?"

The guy's face pinched as he thought. "There was… She had a strawberry birthmark on her inner thigh." He wiped the sweat from his brow as he looked over his shoulder toward the kitchen, checking to make sure that Christina wasn't within earshot.

Alli didn't have a birthmark.

"Is it possible that the birthmark was a bruise or some other kind of mark?" Waylon asked, trying to make sense of exactly what the man was saying.

"No. It was a port-wine mark," Daryl said, making a circle with his fingers on his thigh. "It was about this big. Dark red. She said she had it as a child. She never liked to wear shorts."

Alli lived in shorts in the summertime, or

at least she had. It was possible that she could have been lying to the man about the story, but there was little to no way to replicate a birth-mark like that. Yet Alli did have a tattoo of a small lightning bolt on her ankle.

"Did Sharon," Waylon said, the name sound-ing as foreign as the woman Daryl was describ-ing, "have any tattoos?"

The guy looked up toward the ceiling as though he was trying to find memories on the tiles. "No. Not that I can remember. To be hon-est, she didn't seem the type. She was a bit by the book—if you know what I mean." He gave him a look that told him Daryl wasn't talking about tattoos.

Alli had always been anything but by the book. There was no possible way that the woman Daryl was talking about could have been Waylon's ex-wife. But if it wasn't her, he had no idea who else would have had the ring and the paintings. Maybe it was possible that Alli had given this other woman the items to sell, but something about it all just didn't fit.

He was missing something. He had to be. But what was it that he wasn't seeing?

"And you said that the woman who came to your door was, without a doubt, the same woman you picked up on the side of the road and brought back to Mystery?"

Daryl nodded. "Yep."

"And where did you drop this woman off? Did you bring her back here the first time you met her?"

The sweat dripped on Daryl's brow, and he tried to wipe it away, but it returned just as quickly. "I didn't bring her back here then. She didn't seem like the type who wanted…you know…at least not with me."

"So where did you take her?"

Daryl looked away and tapped his fingers

on the bat in his hands. Everything about his body language screamed that he was trying to come up with a convenient lie, and it made the hairs on the back of Waylon's neck rise. The man hadn't seemed like he really had anything major to hide, but the way he was acting now made him think otherwise.

"Don't bother lying to me," Waylon said, not waiting for the man to answer. "If you do, I will have the police here within minutes."

Daryl gripped the bat and looked back up at him. "I don't want her to get in trouble. I don't want anyone to get in trouble. She seemed like a nice-enough woman."

"She's not *nice enough*," Waylon spat, finally losing his patience with the man's game. "Trust me. We have a reason to believe she may be involved with the kidnapping of a little girl. It's why she needed the money. Why she came to you. So the faster you can give me answers, the faster we can get to that little girl. If you just tell me what you know, maybe we can even save the little girl's life."

"She made me drop her off on the frontage road—about a mile from anything on the north end of town. I don't think she wanted me to know where she was going. She was good at keeping her secrets, you know?" Daryl spoke fast, flustered. "The only thing I can think of is that she kept talking about this ranch. Dunrovin. You know it?"

His stomach sank. "What did she say about it?"

"Only that she was going to take the place down. One person at a time."

"And you thought this woman was innocent?" Christina asked as she walked down the hallway toward them. The glass of water in her hand was shaking. "Where is she, Daryl?

Where can we find her? Where can we find my niece?"

"I don't know anything. I swear, I don't know nothing. All I know is she had some kind of vendetta. I don't know why." Daryl stared at Christina, an apologetic look on his face. "If this were my deal, I would start looking there. At that ranch. Flies are always drawn to things they think are rotten."

Chapter Sixteen

"It has to be Alli. If the woman wasn't Alli, who could it possibly be? Who would want to hurt Winnie? Us?" Christina asked as she tried to keep her rage in check.

None of this made any sense. Winnie was innocent in all this. Alli was the only person who could have wanted her—she was the only one with any motivation to do it. That was, unless Daryl had been right and the person behind Winnie's disappearance had been carrying a vendetta toward the ranch and everyone who lived there.

It felt like they were chasing a ghost—a ghost who knew their weakest points.

Everyone loved Winnie. If a person wanted to hurt everyone at the ranch, the girl was the best place to start. She was the heart of the place and everyone in it.

Waylon reached over and took Christina's hand, gripping it hard as he pressed down on the gas. Her body flew back in the seat as he raced the truck back toward the ranch. "I don't have a frigging clue why this person did what she did. But whoever this woman is, she's not going to get away with anything else. And if she touches a single hair on Winnie's head, I will make it my mission in life to make sure she never draws another breath."

His words carried the weight of truth to them.

"You don't really think this mystery woman would hurt a child, do you?"

"Don't underestimate people. Evil is evil.

And truly evil people, they don't have a sense of right or wrong. They believe whatever they do is right. For all we know, this woman is psychotic, or a sociopath. She's capable of anything."

She leaned over to read the speedometer on the truck—the needle pointed at seventy. "Can't you drive any faster?"

He slammed his foot down on the gas pedal, and the truck bellowed. They squealed down the road, and the ranch quickly came into view. The parking lot was full of flashing red and blue lights, and people were milling around the barn. Even the horses were alarmed, and as they drove past the pasture, a mare raced down the fence line next to them—almost as if the horse knew who was missing and feared what could have happened to Winnie just as much as they did.

It was amazing how quickly the love for a

child could bring even the most unlikely people together.

Christina squeezed Waylon's fingers. She needed him, and she had a feeling he needed her just as badly. It was inconvenient and unwieldy, but she loved him. Looking at him, the intensity in his gaze, the strength in his body and soul, she loved everything about him. No matter where in the world he went, or what the future would bring, she would love him. She hated it, but there was no fighting the truth deep in her heart.

Mrs. Fitzgerald ran up to the truck as they struggled to find a parking spot in the melee of emergency vehicles. There was even an ambulance parked toward the edge of the parking lot. The EMTs were standing among the police officers, and everyone had a look of concern on their face.

Waylon let go of her hand and rolled down the window as his mother stopped beside them. "We're organizing search parties. We're going to go over every square inch of this place. Wyatt is setting up a grid in and around Mystery, and the highway patrols are watching all roads. Everyone is helping. Everyone," Eloise said, her voice cracking with nerves.

Waylon jumped out of the truck and drew his mother into his embrace. Christina followed him. "Don't worry, Mom. We'll find her. They couldn't have gotten far. How's Gwen doing?"

Eloise pointed a shaking finger across the yard toward Gwen, who was sitting on the porch steps. She was moving back and forth, hugging herself. Wyatt was with her, rubbing her back, but he was talking to one of the officers.

"She's doing just about as well as you'd expect," Eloise said. "If something's happened..."

"Don't go there, Mom," Waylon said, his voice firm with resolve. "She's going to be okay."

Christina doubted what he said was true, but she nodded. They needed to be the backbone of the family; they needed to stay strong so everyone around them could as well.

"What did Gwen say? Did she see the woman who took Winnie or anything?" Christina asked.

"She's having a hard time processing everything. She said she didn't see anything—one minute Winnie was in her house at the edge of Dunrovin with her, playing with her toys, and the next minute she was gone. Wyatt said there weren't even any tire marks in the gravel or signs someone had driven up to their trailer. He's thinking that either the person responsible is still somewhere on the ranch or there may have been more than one person involved."

The thought made Christina stop. "How many are involved?"

Eloise shrugged. "At this point we don't know."

Christina looked over at Waylon. His lips were puckered and the lines of his frown seemed deeper than ever before. "What if Alli wasn't even the one driving her car? Think about it. She may have never even left this town."

"Or she could have gone south. She could have hitchhiked to Mexico by now."

"Or she could be...dead." Eloise covered her mouth. "I'm so sorry, Christina. I shouldn't have said it."

"No," Christina whispered, stunned. "Alli isn't dead. She can't be dead. She's probably with Winnie right now. Wyatt's probably right. Maybe Alli had someone working with her, someone she convinced to drive her car. And take Winnie." Even as she spoke, she knew how far-fetched the whole thing sounded.

Alli wasn't the kind who normally kept a throng of female friends. If she had one named Sharon, Christina would have thought she would have heard about the woman at least in passing from her sister before she had disappeared. Then again, maybe she wouldn't have. Her life was nothing if not a jumbled mess of dangerous secrets.

IT WASN'T HIS first search party, but it was the first one in which Waylon thought there was hope they'd find the victim alive. That hope might be misplaced, but he couldn't bring himself to believe anything else.

No matter how hard he tried to compartmentalize his feelings, there was no escaping the emotional reality that it was his daughter's life at stake.

As his team moved through the pasture, their motion made some of the dry, light snowflakes rise in the air. It was almost as if the snow was floating upward, disobeying the laws of nature and following only its own desire to get back to the safety of the sky. If only it was that simple to escape the constant beating life wrought.

One of the police officers Wyatt had sent with them flagged him down. "Mr. Fitzgerald, does this belong to your daughter?" The man lifted up a pink hooded sweatshirt with Dora the Explorer on the back. Its sleeve was stretched a bit, like it had been pulled over the girl's Ace bandage.

Waylon didn't want to admit that he didn't know his child well enough to know what kind of clothing she wore, or even if she liked Dora or not, so he looked to Christina. She gave him a small, almost imperceptible nod instead of calling him out in front of the group of rescuers.

"Yeah," Waylon said, rushing over to the deputy.

A sense of relief flooded him. Finally, they had a clue to Winnie's whereabouts—and proof that she might still be on the ranch. Now it was just a matter of finding her in the nearly thousand acres of the place.

The sweatshirt was partially frozen where it had been lying on the ground and covered by a thin layer of snow, and as the deputy turned it around, on the left breast, Waylon noticed a brown dot of dried blood. He looked over his shoulder to Christina. The pink in her cheeks disappeared, and her mouth fell open as her gaze moved over the shirt in the deputy's hands.

"It's probably not hers," Waylon said, stepping between Christina and the sweatshirt. "If she's anything like me, maybe she bit her attacker. My girl would fight."

Christina just stared at him like she could

still see the sweatshirt through his body. "We have to find her, Waylon. We have to find her right now."

She started to move again, pacing around the area, searching the ground. It didn't make him feel any better that she was no longer looking up; instead, everyone was now looking for more blood on the ground.

He tried to ignore the sick feeling in his stomach. Winnie wasn't hurt. She couldn't be hurt. He would save her. He *had* to save her, or he could never go on. He could never face a world that would take his daughter away from him the same week that she'd come into his life.

Christina slipped her hand into his, and he realized that he had been standing there in silence as everyone else had started to move again, except the deputy who'd found the sweatshirt, who was documenting the scene and taking pictures.

"Let's go," Christina said, her voice soft but resolute and strong. "She needs you. You can't stop now. We have to hurry."

He followed her into the pasture, and they started moving again. Ahead of them was a small embankment. They slowly picked their way up the hill. Some of the dry grass had been trampled down where cows had moved through the area to the stock pond on the other side of the hill. He scanned the area, but aside from the cows' tracks, there was nothing to tell them that any other humans had been in the area recently.

Yet he knew she had to be close. He could almost feel her. It was strange to think that this little girl could now have such a pull on his heart. As he thought about Winnie, Christina and his family, he realized how alone he had been when he'd been away from the ranch. Part of him had been missing—the love of his family, a love as big as the sky over Montana.

He moved ahead of Christina and to the top of the hill. Cattails and weeds surrounded the stock pond, and some of the weeds were at least a few feet tall. Animals coming in for a drink had pushed some of the vegetation down, and bits of the detritus floated in the water. The trail that led down from where he stood had once been mud, but it was now frozen solid by the harsh, cold winds of winter.

It was odd to think that Christmas was only just around the corner. Winnie had been talking about it almost incessantly every time they had been alone. According to her, she wanted nothing more than a puppy.

He smiled at the thought of his mother's reaction if he showed up at their door on Christmas Eve carrying a puppy, complete with a big red bow. His mother would undoubtedly be mad, furious even, that he had brought another animal to the ranch, but she could never resist an animal in need—especially an animal that wagged its tail and promised licks.

It broke his heart as he looked out at the pond and was met with the rattle of dry grass and the lonely whisper of a long winter. Winnie needed the Christmas of her dreams. She deserved to be loved and cared for. To get everything she ever wanted. If only they could find her. They had to find her. She had to be safe.

"Waylon," Christina said, her voice choked. "Look." She motioned toward the far side of the pond, where a patch of weeds leaned over the water. She took off running in that direction. He took a few steps after her before he saw the blue fabric bobbing in the water near the bank.

From the distance, he couldn't tell exactly what the fabric was, or what it was covering.

He sprinted after Christina.

It couldn't be Winnie. It couldn't be. No.

She hadn't been gone that long. Only about an hour. No one would want to kill the girl.

He didn't want to believe anyone would be crazy enough to hurt a child, but he knew all too well what people were capable of. He could only hope his gut was wrong—and his daughter was just fine and probably hiding in the weeds somewhere on the ranch, somewhere far away from the horror in front of him.

He rushed past Christina. She couldn't get there first. He had to shield her from whatever they were about to find.

"Go call the rest of the team," he ordered, but she paid him no mind. In fact, she didn't even slow down as she chased after him on the uneven path that led to the far side of the pond.

"Winnie!" she called, terror in her voice.

It wasn't his daughter bobbing there in the water like one of the weeds. It couldn't be. It just couldn't be.

He rushed down the steep bank and ran straight into the water. It was cold and ice had collected on the edges of the bank, but he barely noticed the bite. He reached into the water. In one solid motion he flipped over the body. It was Winnie.

Her little eyes were closed, and her lips were blue. Her skin wasn't mottled, and as he pressed his fingers against her neck, he could almost make out a sluggish pulse.

He pulled her from the water and carried her up onto the bank as he let his training take over. He started chest compressions.

"Come on, Winnie. Come on, baby." He pressed down. One. Two. Three. Four. "Come on, baby. Daddy's here. Breathe for me."

He pressed five more times. The little girl didn't move.

It was impossible to know how long she had been floating in the water, but if there was any higher power, they wouldn't let her die. She was just a child. She didn't deserve to pay the price for his mistakes. She had to live. She had to.

Christina fell to her knees beside the girl and held the fingers that stuck out from the end of the girl's bandage. "Come on, Winnie girl. Come on. Breathe for us."

He did another set of compressions on Winnie's chest, hoping like he'd never hoped before that the action would be enough to pull her back to the land of the living—to a world where they could be together. All three of them.

"Please, baby, please. I need you," he begged. "I love you. Please. Stay with Daddy."

Winnie's eyelashes fluttered, and water poured from her mouth. She coughed and gagged as she forced the fluid from her lungs. She moved to sit up, but her tiny body was so weak that she fell back to the ground.

He picked her up and pulled her into the

safety of his arms. "I'm so sorry, Winnie. I'm so sorry, baby. Don't worry. Daddy's got you," he cooed as she coughed and sputtered on his shoulder.

He stood up as he looked over at Christina. "She's going to make it. We got her. We got her, honey."

Tears streamed down Christina's cheeks. "Now we just have to find the person responsible. They have to pay."

Chapter Seventeen

Christina couldn't stop watching Waylon and the way he hovered over Winnie as the emergency room nurse wrapped her in a warm blanket.

"Mr. Fitzgerald, you need to back up. I need to check her vitals," the nurse ordered.

Waylon stared at the nurse, and *shooting daggers* didn't even seem strong enough to describe the way he looked at the woman.

"Okay," the nurse said, not waiting for him to speak. "It's okay if you stay with the girl, but—"

"She's not just any girl. This is my daughter," he argued. "And I'm not going anywhere. I'm not leaving her again. Not until I know she's safe."

"She's safe in this hospital, sir," the nurse said, clearly not getting the message.

Christina moved closer to Waylon and took his hand as she glanced toward the nurse. "No one except hospital staff is allowed anywhere near the girl, do you understand?"

The nurse raised an eyebrow, almost as if she were surprised to be taken on by both Christina and Waylon, but instead of arguing, this time she answered with a nod. "I will have security come over and stand guard beside the door. No one will be allowed to come or go. I promise. But for right now, I need you both out of this room. You've done a great job in getting this girl to this point, but now she needs the help only this hospital and I can provide."

"Thank you, Nurse. Thank you." Christina pulled Waylon along by the arm. "Come on, honey. Come on. She'll be okay."

"I can't… I can't leave her," he said. "She needs us." He motioned toward Winnie.

His daughter's chest was rising and falling with the sleep of the exhausted.

"Don't worry, honey. She's going to be okay. They have her. Security is on their way. Don't forget, whoever is responsible for this—they're still out there. We need to find them. We have to stop them before they have the chance to do anything this horrible again."

Outside Winnie's room, they were surrounded by a sea of brown and black uniforms. There were at least ten police officers, both highway patrol and sheriff's deputies, milling around the unit. Near the entrance were Gwen and Wyatt, who rushed over as they noticed Waylon and Christina coming out of Winnie's room.

"Is she going to be okay?" Gwen asked. Her eyes were red and her skin blotchy from what must have been hours of crying.

Christina nodded. "She's alive. They are trying to get her warmed up and rested."

"Did she say anything about who was behind this? About what she saw?" Wyatt asked, looking toward Waylon.

Waylon stared out into space and slowly shook his head. "She's just lucky to be alive. We're lucky we found her in time."

"Our guys are still going over the scene," Wyatt said. He reached into his pocket, pulled out his cell phone and opened a picture. He handed the phone to Christina. "But they managed to find the missing paperwork stuffed under a rock just inside the water's edge."

"What? Why would anyone do that?" she asked, staring at the picture of the papers under the water.

"I have no idea, but you think if they were after money, they would have simply sold the papers. Something like a passport can go for a lot of money on the black market," Wyatt said. "Sometimes they even use things like that for transporting kids across the border illegally."

Chills ran down her spine. Why were so many people determined to exploit kids? She must have lived in another world, because things like that didn't even cross her mind—not in the middle of Montana.

Several nurses and a doctor rushed into Winnie's room, and the people standing in the ER grew quiet. Another of the ER doctors, who had been standing at the nurses' station, looked over at them and slowly made his way over.

"Are you the parents of Winnie Bell?" he asked, motioning to Waylon and Christina.

She didn't really know how to respond. She wasn't the girl's mother, and now that Waylon had claimed his daughter, she wasn't really even the guardian.

"We are," Waylon said, squeezing her hand. "What can we do for you?"

The doctor gave them a weak but reassuring smile. "I heard about what happened. Don't worry. Every year we get a child who falls through the ice. We're practiced dealing with situations like this. The great thing about kids is that they are so resilient. From what I saw, you got to her just in time. If she's a fighter, she'll make it through this."

"She's a fighter," Waylon said.

"I'm glad to hear it," the doctor said with a thankful nod. "Now, about you both. How are you doing?"

"We're fine. We aren't the ones who were floating in the water," Waylon said, glancing over at the room where his daughter lay.

The doctor lifted Waylon's arm and pushed

up the sleeve of his shirt. For the first time, Christina noticed red welts on his skin, covered in what looked like little pustules.

Waylon pulled his arm from the doctor's grip. "Don't worry, I'm fine." He pushed down his sleeve.

"Where did you guys say you found the little girl?" the doctor asked.

Wyatt stepped forward. "Does it matter?"

"Oh, no, don't get me wrong," the doctor said with a slight wave. "It's just that a rash like that is uncommon this time of year. Though—"

"I've been stressed. It's probably just hives or something," Waylon interrupted.

"No. A rash like this…" he said, taking Waylon's arm. The doctor touched the skin around the red welts. "These are from some kind of allergic reaction." He leaned in closer to take a better look. "It looks like poison ivy."

"We don't have poison ivy here. We're too far north."

"No, I know. It's probably something in the same family, maybe stinging nettles." The doctor leaned back and frowned for a moment. "Actually, I had a case just like this a few days ago. A woman came in presenting the same symptoms."

She had seen something like this before, on a ranch hand's Labrador retriever. The dog had been playing near the stock pond and had gotten into some kind of stinging underbrush.

"Who was the woman who came in with the rash?" Christina asked, more than aware that HIPAA laws, the restrictions that required medical confidentiality, would prohibit the man from answering. Yet she had to try.

"You know I can't answer that. I can't give you names."

A nurse walked out from Winnie's room and

made her way over toward them. "Dr. Nay?" she asked, motioning toward the doctor standing with them. "Dr. Rogers needs your help."

The doctor looked back to Christina. "I'm sorry I can't be of more help."

"Don't worry," Wyatt said. "We'll be back, warrant in hand. If there's even a chance the woman you treated is the same woman responsible for Winnie's attack, the judge will give me anything I want."

"I look forward to helping," the doctor said, turning away to go to the room. "For now, you'll have to be satisfied that we are going to make sure Winnie's well taken care of. And," he said, motioning toward Waylon's arm, "you might want to take some Benadryl and lather that up with calamine lotion. If you take care of it, your rash should be gone within a few days."

"Thanks, Doc," Waylon said. His shoulders fell and there was an air of resignation in his voice. Christina felt the same way, for once again it was as if, when they finally started to make progress, everything in the world stood in their way.

She understood the need for privacy and HIPAA regulations. She did. However, it didn't make it any easier when it impeded their progress in the investigation. They needed to find the woman with the rash.

No one went out to that stock pond at this time of year. No one—unless they were trying to hide something. Maybe Alli had been there, scoping out a place where she could kill Winnie. Or maybe she had been spending her nights at the place. It was well out of view from the staff at the ranch house and the vacationers who came and went from the guest houses and close enough that she could come and go unnoticed while she was waiting for her opportunity to take Winnie.

Christina could almost feel the pieces clicking together.

She couldn't wait to see her sister again. To confront her about what she had done and what she had put the family through. Perhaps she could even get some much-needed answers from her.

The nurse cleared her throat as she motioned to Waylon's arm. "That's a doozy of a rash," the nurse said. "The doctor's right, you definitely want to take care of it. My cousin had a rash like that a few days ago."

Her cousin?

Waylon's eyes lit up. "Oh, yeah?" he asked. "What's your cousin's name?"

"Lisa. Lisa Chase. Why?" the nurse asked, oblivious to what the doctor had been talking about—and the HIPAA laws that had stood in their way.

"Did she come in here to be treated?" Wyatt pressed her.

The nurse frowned. "Yeah. Dr. Nay told her exactly what he just told you. Benadryl and calamine. At this stage, with just the pustules and no oozing lesions, it's the only thing you want to do. The next step is antibiotics if you've been scratching at them and they become infected."

Waylon nodded, but as he looked over at Christina, she could tell he wasn't really listening to anything the nurse had to say; instead, he was shifting his weight from one foot to the other just like a runner getting ready for a sprint.

"Thanks," Waylon said, "I'll get right on that."

"If you need, I bet I can get the doctor to prescribe—"

"No. I'm fine." He took Christina's hand and

gave it a squeeze. They had answers. They finally had some kind of an answer.

"Wyatt?" he asked, turning away from the nurse.

His brother had a gleam in his eye. "I'll have my men stay here with Winnie. She'll be protected by at least three officers at all times in addition to the hospital's security."

It was really no wonder that both the brothers had gone into law enforcement—they knew how to keep a person at ease even when the world was falling apart.

Chapter Eighteen

Hate wasn't a new emotion in her world. No, it was a feeling Christina had become well versed in when she had watched her parents fight, when they had torn at one another, and the day her sister had repeated their cycle—and left her holding the strings to a life that she had never intended on leading. Yet she had never hated anyone or anything more than she hated Lisa Chase in that moment.

The woman had tried to kill one of the few people she truly loved.

She stared out the window as they pulled into William Poe's driveway.

Why did everything always come back to this vile man? He was like a poison. First Bianca, then Monica and Alli, and now they could even tie him to Lisa. He had always proclaimed his innocence—so far, he'd even been cleared of any wrongdoing in each of the cases, but he could only run for so long before the authorities would catch him playing in the shadows. Or at least, Christina hoped.

Then again, maybe he wasn't anything more than just a man who had the power to make women go crazy. She followed Wyatt and Waylon up to the front door of the evil man's house. Knowing her luck, he probably wasn't even home. He had a knack of being out of town when it came to the crimes that were rocking the community of Mystery.

Wyatt banged on the door. The sound was hollow and eerie.

A slight wheeze escaped her throat.

"What?" Waylon asked, taking her hand.

"Nothing," she said, and as the word ghosted from her lips, the front door opened.

Standing there was William Poe. He looked a bit haggard and tired, but his suit jacket was crisp from being freshly laundered and pressed. "What is it now?" he grumbled.

"Is your friend Lisa Chase here?" Wyatt asked.

"Why would you need to see her? She's done nothing." William's face contorted with rage. "I don't know what kind of thing you have against me or why, but this has to stop. You can't keep harassing me. This is ridiculous."

"We're harassing you?" Christina said, nearly hissing the words in her fury. "Ever since you entered our lives, everything has been going wrong. People have been killing each other, going missing, and stealing and hurting children."

"You think any of this has to do with me?" William laughed, the sound low and menacing. "You are just as crazy as your sister if you think I want to have anything to do with any of that or with any of you. Have you ever stopped to think that where everything truly stops and ends is at your family's goddamned ranch?"

"Shut your mouth," Waylon seethed.

"No. You all need to be put out of business— you and your family have only brought trouble to this community. And once you're gone, that cursed guest ranch will be sold to the highest bidder. I'd be doing a public service if I got to be the one to take you all down."

"Is that a threat?" Wyatt asked, his voice even more dangerous than Poe's.

"Ha ha ha." William laughed, the sound as cheap and ridiculous as his suit. "I don't make threats. When I say I'm going to do something, I won't stop until it's done."

"How dare you think you can come at my family? My home?" Christina lunged toward the man, but Waylon grabbed her by the arms and pulled her back.

"Not here. Not now. Wyatt's going to handle this," he whispered, the sound harsh in her ear. "If you touch a hair on that man's head, we will lose any ground we have in going after him."

"We're not here to pick a fight with you, Poe. We're only here to speak to Lisa. Now, is she here or not?" Wyatt continued.

"Why in the hell would I tell you?" Poe sneered.

"If you don't help us, I have no problem getting more police and media involved. One little call and you and your personal life will be out in the open. I'd hate it if some pictures of you and one of your many female acquaintances would make it into the hands of a reporter or two."

"Now who's threatening?" William growled. "How dare you come here and treat me like I'm some kind of criminal. I haven't done a god-damned thing."

"If it walks like a duck." Wyatt shrugged.

Waylon leaned in close to Christina so only she could hear him speak. "What photos is Wyatt talking about?" he whispered.

She turned to him and cupped his ear. "They found a set of incriminating photos when they were investigating Bianca's murder. There was one with Alli in a lace teddy."

Waylon sent her a look of surprise but then turned back to his brother and Poe. "I am sure the press would love to get their hands on the information that links you to Alli. Especially after everything that's happened."

"If those pictures are leaked, I will come after you. I will sue you and the sheriff's department for every penny—"

"Oh, don't misunderstand me, Poe. I have no intention of misconduct. However, I'm sure there are more copies of those photos we found," Wyatt continued.

It was a wonderful thing to watch the brothers work.

"That's ridiculous. Alli and I were done a long time ago."

Christina glanced over at Wyatt, but he didn't give anything away.

"Do you know where Alli is?" Christina asked, unable to hold herself back any longer. "I need to find my sister."

William turned to look at her. "Why do you think I'd give two shakes about what has come of your sister?"

The way he said the words made her unsettled. It was almost as if there was something he knew that she didn't—something sinister.

"What *has* come of my sister, Poe?" she seethed.

He laughed again, the sound filled with mirth. "I told you. Your sister is of no concern to me. She's been nothing but a thorn in my side ever since—"

"You threw her to the curb?" she interrupted. "You know, I have had a hard time understanding why my sister has done the things she has in the last few months, but now—talking to you for just a few minutes—I can almost understand why she was driven to the edges of her sanity."

Poe stepped closer, pressing his face close to hers. "Maybe you should look to yourself before you start pointing fingers at me, little girl."

Waylon's hands tightened on her arms.

"Before someone—namely you—gets hurt here, Poe, where's Lisa?" Wyatt said, motioning inside the man's house. "For once, take a moment and make a choice that will serve you the best in the end."

Poe took a few steps back and looked back over his shoulder, like he was looking for the woman in question.

"You know you don't love her. You don't love anyone but yourself. So, before you are pulled any deeper into our investigation, get out. Get her to come and talk to us," Wyatt pressed.

Poe said something Christina couldn't quite hear, but from the look on his face as he glanced back at them, she was glad she couldn't. "Lisa!" William called. "Get your ass out here, woman! The little deputy and his goon squad want to ask you some questions."

A small, dark-haired woman, the one she had seen the other day, stepped into the doorway.

"Don't speak to them. In the meantime, I'm calling my lawyer."

"For me?" the small woman squeaked.

William laughed, and the sound echoed off the walls of the house. "Hardly. Whatever mess you are in, you are in it by yourself. I can't be associated with any more trouble." He stopped and pointed toward the brothers. "And I'm sure that no pictures will go public. I've played your stupid game. Do we all have an understanding?"

Waylon glared at the man. "One thing we will never have, Poe, is an understanding. I don't want you to think for one minute that we see you as anything more than the societal louse that you are."

Wyatt laughed as Poe stormed off down the hall. "Louse? That's the best you got for that guy?"

Waylon shrugged. "I would have called him an ass—"

"Stop," Lisa squeaked. "William may not be a perfect man, but he doesn't deserve to be talked

about like that. Especially not by a civil ser-
vant," she said, pointing at the badge on Wyatt's
uniform. "Your job is to protect the innocent."

Wyatt laughed. "Poe is far from innocent."

"Of course he is." Lisa looked around the
driveway like a trapped animal as she scratched
at the welts that ran up and down her arms.

"What makes you think he's innocent?"
Wyatt asked.

"I'm the one who killed them. He never
wanted me to hurt a hair on their heads. But I
had to do what needed to be done. One must
sacrifice for the greater good."

"Who did you kill?" Wyatt asked, his voice
as cold as the snow on the ground around them.

"Alli was first." Lisa looked at Wyatt, but her
expression was vacant—indifferent.

Christina's ears rang with the woman's words.

"You *killed* Alli?" Christina whispered, the

words like weights that made her sink to her knees as they left her body.

"She had it coming. She was no innocent. The little girl, on the other hand, that was unfortunate. I didn't want to kill her. She just wouldn't come quietly. She kept trying to scream. Especially when I told her how I was going to sell her."

"You were going to sell my daughter?" Waylon seethed.

Lisa nodded, like the trafficking of children was among the most normal things in the world. "I would have been set up for life." She glanced over her shoulder and in the direction where Poe had disappeared. "I don't want to have to depend on anyone too much. Dependence leads to disaster." She turned back and leered at Christina. "Just ask your sister."

"Where is she? Where's Alli? What did you do with her?"

Lisa looked over at her. "How could you find one without the other? I went out of my way to make sure that mother and daughter could at least be together in the afterlife."

"How could you?" Christina started to lunge toward Lisa, but Waylon stopped her.

"How could I what? Kill your sister?" Lisa looked utterly confused, the face of a monster. "Don't worry. It was one quick bullet to the head. It was just like shooting out my tire. It was easy." She reached behind her and pulled out a gun. "In fact, it was just like this," she said, raising it and pointing the barrel toward Christina.

Before she had time to react, Waylon was on the woman, pushing her to the floor and pulling the weapon from her hands.

Blood streamed from Lisa's nose as she looked up at Christina. She laughed. The sound was high and crazed. "I may not have gotten you, but your day is coming. All of your days are coming. I may not be the one pulling the trigger, but you're all going to die."

Waylon rolled Lisa over, pressing his knee into the center of the woman's back as he pulled her arms behind her. "That won't happen. I will stop at nothing to protect the ones I love."

Chapter Nineteen

She wasn't merely broken. No, Christina was destroyed, and all Waylon could do was hold her. He held her as they'd watched Wyatt cuff Lisa and stuff her into his car. He'd held her when they heard about her sister's body being pulled from the pond. And he held her as they lay in his bed and stared up at the ceiling.

If he had his way, he'd hold her forever.

She'd barely spoken all night, and he hadn't even mentioned eating.

Christina shifted in his arms, and her loose hair slipped over his chest. He ran his fingers through her locks in a feeble attempt to comfort her in the only way he knew how. There was no going back and undoing what had been done, or taking back the tragedy that seemed to have become a constant in not just their lives but those of all who lived and worked at Dunrovin.

She moved slightly and looked up at him. "What are you going to do?"

"What do you mean?"

"When are you leaving?" She sat up a bit more and lifted herself onto her elbow so they were eye to eye.

He cupped her face, running his thumb over the soft skin of her cheek. "I will stay here as long as you need me."

She snorted. "We both know that can't happen. You've given your life to the army. They are going to want you back sometime."

He smiled, but the ache that had filled his

heart—the one that had started the moment he'd realized his feelings toward her were more than mere friendship—expanded and threatened to make his chest explode.

"I have a couple more days here, but when I leave, you and Winnie…you can come back to Fort Bragg with me."

Christina looked out the window, where the bits of falling snow were shining like glitter in the moon's silver light. "I don't think it's a good idea to take Winnie away from this ranch. This is the only home she's known. She's already been through so much change." She looked back at him, a tear in her eye. "But ultimately the choice is yours. She's your daughter."

"Alli chose you to watch over her, to take care of her. She didn't choose me."

The tear slipped down her cheek. "What Alli wanted, or thought…it doesn't matter now."

"Yes, it does. She chose you because she

knew what a good mom you would be. She chose you because you are a good person. She loved you. Just like I love you."

Christina's mouth opened with surprise, and she made a muffled, strangled sound, as though she wasn't sure what to say.

"Don't say anything at all," he said, filling the emotional gap between them. "You don't have to love me. I don't want you to feel like you need to say anything. Whether or not you love me, I love you. I love everything about you—your strength, the way you put Winnie and the needs of others before yourself. You're so selfless. So giving. You are one of the kindest people I've met in my entire life. I would be a fool not to love you."

"No," she said. "I'd be a fool not to love you." She leaned in and kissed him.

His body awoke, just as it always did when

she was near. As their lips parted, he stared into her eyes, and a piece of his heart broke.

She loved him.

He loved her.

Yet there was too much between them to make anything work. Sometimes love just wasn't enough to bring two people together.

She'd never leave this place.

"I'm scared," she said, laying her head back down on his chest.

The words, though barely above a whisper, reverberated through him as though she had screamed them.

"Why? What are you scared of?" he asked, wrapping his arms around her.

"I'm scared of what the future will bring. And I'm scared of losing you." She reached up and took his hand, her ring flashing in the silver light streaming in from the window.

"I have to go back to work, it's true." He sighed. "But like I said, you and Winnie can come with me. Take a break for a week and get out of this place. You can check out the base. Then we can come back for Christmas."

"Then what?" she asked. "Whether or not we like the base isn't the issue."

He knew what she was saying was right, and he knew the answer—an answer that would change his life forever. When he'd come to the ranch, his career had been everything to him, but now, in a matter of days, Christina and Winnie had become the center of his life and the only things that filled his heart.

"I only have a few months left. I don't have to reenlist. When I get out, I can come back here. We can set up a house. We can get married."

"Get married?" She wiped the remnants of the tears from her cheek as she smiled up at him.

He took her right hand and pulled her grandmother's ring from her finger. "If you don't

want this ring, we can get another one, but…"
He sat up slightly, but she wouldn't let him go.
"Don't you want me to get down on one knee?"

She laughed, and the light from the moon
filled her eyes. "The ring is perfect. And you
are crazy if you think that, even for one minute, I'm going to let you go."

His laughter blanketed hers, and he kissed
the top of her head. "So does that mean you
will marry me?"

She sat up and moved on top of him, strad-
dling him between her thighs. "Say it again.
Something that good I want to hear twice," she
said with an excited giggle.

He lifted her left hand and poised the ring to
slip it on her finger. "Ms. Christina Bell, though
this may be fast, I know with all my heart that
I want to spend every waking moment with
you. I never want to spend another day apart.
And though life may get in the way and draw

us in separate directions, I want to always come home to you. No matter where home is."

"Do you promise to not always be Mr. Serious?" She smiled. "And to love me unconditionally?"

"Always."

"Then, yes. Yes, Waylon Fitzgerald, I will be yours. Forever."

Regardless of everything that was going on in their lives or at the ranch, for one moment he was completely and blissfully happy. All the fears that had filled him, all of his apprehension and scars from the past were just that—in the past. Moving forward, they could have their fairy tale.

* * * * *

MILLS & BOON®
Large Print – November 2017

ROMANCE

The Pregnant Kavakos Bride	Sharon Kendrick
The Billionaire's Secret Princess	Caitlin Crews
Sicilian's Baby of Shame	Carol Marinelli
The Secret Kept from the Greek	Susan Stephens
A Ring to Secure His Crown	Kim Lawrence
Wedding Night with Her Enemy	Melanie Milburne
Salazar's One-Night Heir	Jennifer Hayward
The Mysterious Italian Houseguest	Scarlet Wilson
Bound to Her Greek Billionaire	Rebecca Winters
Their Baby Surprise	Katrina Cudmore
The Marriage of Inconvenience	Nina Singh

HISTORICAL

Ruined by the Reckless Viscount	Sophia James
Cinderella and the Duke	Janice Preston
A Warriner to Rescue Her	Virginia Heath
Forbidden Night with the Warrior	Michelle Willingham
The Foundling Bride	Helen Dickson

MEDICAL

Mummy, Nurse...Duchess?	Kate Hardy
Falling for the Foster Mum	Karin Baine
The Doctor and the Princess	Scarlet Wilson
Miracle for the Neurosurgeon	Lynne Marshall
English Rose for the Sicilian Doc	Annie Claydon
Engaged to the Doctor Sheikh	Meredith Webber

1017 GEN STD LP